prince
madog

"Drink, my dear lord, and listen to this new chaunt that Doag has for you."

prince madog

discoverer of america
a legendary story

BY JOAN DANE

ILLUSTRATED BY A.S. BOYD

HESPERUS

Published by Hesperus Press
167-169 Great Portland Street,
London, W1W 5PF
www.hesperus.press

First published by Elliot Stock in 1909
This edition first published by Hesperus Press in 2024
© Hesperus Press
Illustrations by Alexander Stuart Boyle

Edited by Katy B.
Design by Roland Codd
Printed and bound in the United Kingdom by Bell & Bain Ltd, Glasgow

ISBN 978-1-84391-930-8
e-ISBN 978-1-84391-931-5

ꝺeꝺıcaꞇıon

I DEDICATE THIS BOOK
TO THE WEISHMEN OF AMERICA AND BRITAIN,
AND TO ONE WHO HAS ALREADY PASSED
TO THE ISLANDS OF THE BLEST.

JOAN DANE

preface

The Chronicle of Madog of Gwynedd is no fairy tale, but a story founded on extracts taken from the manuscripts of the Abbeys of Strata Florida and Conway; where, were kept, the records of the chief historical events of the Welsh nation; records where were compared with each other, every three years, by the most influential Bards of the country.

Henry VII, we can but surmise, was acquainted with the story, for Guthin Owen (whom he had commissioned to trace the Tudor pedigree), had made a copy of the Strata Florida manuscript – if unacquainted with it, why, when still insecure upon the English throne, should he, parsimonious and cautious as he is known to have been, have instructed Bartholomew Columbus (Who was begging on his brother's behalf) to send Christopher to him with his plans and charts, when the rest of the world but jeered at his hair-brained schemes? – unless he had something better to go upon than the visionary imagination of a poor sea-captain!

If fate had not ordained otherwise, it might surely have been English gold and English enterprise that had fitted out the fleet which discovered the New World!

But alas! Bartholomew, on his return journey with the promises of the English King, was captured by pirates, imprisoned for a long period, reaching Spain only to find his brother had already sailed!

In the year 1477 (fifteen years before Columbus started on voyage) we find a poem of Sir Meredyth ap Rhys, eulogizing Madog's expedition.

And amongst many other bardic verses may be found mention of the same event.

The legend – as told to the Spaniards by the Aztecs of their god, Quetzalcoatl,[1] tallies well with what is known of the Welsh Prince who came to them from unknown regions, three hundred years previously – whose return the Aztecs confessed to be still awaiting, for had they not mistaken the Spaniards for him and his retainers!

Quetzalcoatl … whose emblem was the Bird Serpent[2] he who had crossed the seas from the land of Tlapallan,

---

1. Prescott's *History of Mexico*

2. Bird serpent, or Griffin of Wales

leaving again, it is true, many years after ... home-sick for the land of his fathers! But promising to return!

"He is of tall stature, white skin, long dark hair and flowing beard ... he who instructed the natives in the use of metals, agriculture and the arts of government,"[3] was non other than the deified Welsh Prince, who sought peace in a country, far removed from the blood-stained soil of Wales.

There is today a tribe of American Indians known as the Madagwys, or Doags, of fair complexion, speaking a language akin to Welsh, a tribe who aver their progenitors came from Gwynedd, a tribe possessing manuscripts in large cipher, sewn (for preservation) in otter skin.[4]

In the year 1669, one Morgan Jones was captured by Indians, and was about to be put to death, when offering his last prayer in his native Welsh, he was overheard by one of the chiefs, who understanding, came and spoke to him; subsequently offering a ransom to the headman for himself and his companions and treating them with great kindness.[5]

Columbus, Franciscus, Lopez, and others of the Spaniards wondered at finding amongst the natives reverence for the Cross, the use of beads, and many rudiments of the Christian religion! Till Cortez asking Montezuma the reason, he answered – "Many years ago, a strange nation came from

---

3. Prescott's *Mexico*

4. *An Inquiry concerning the First Discovery of America.* J. Williams, 1791

5. *British Remains.* Pub. 1777

across the seas, a civil nation, from whom (he had heard his father aver) he and most of his chiefs were descended."[6]

Legends die hard – because there is in every one some vital spark of truth! Thus, we read, as fairy tales, of "Islands of the Blest", of "Gardens of Hesperides", "Lands beyond the Setting Sun!"

Legend says. . . a flood once downed the world … *their* world … that Western Continent, I trow, which was the cradle of the human race … an Atlantis! … Hesperides! … what you will, lying today, perhaps, beneath the waters of the Gulf of Mexico!

No doubt some vast seismic disturbance rent the earth, from whose fury only a few escaped in barques of various build … borne eastwards, stranded, perhaps, on Ararat, or on the more lofty mountains of Bactriana!

And what more probable, than that those human waifs, should hand down from generation to generation the story of their father's land, and that the homing instinct should make them ever long again to travel westward , that, perad-venture some day, they themselves might see the country of which they inherited such happy recollection!

From Asia, through Europe, westwards – legend says – swept the great Celtic tribes … leaving their hallmark, circles of stone (emblem of their sun-god Baal) upon the plains of Persia

6. Prescott's *Mexico*

... upon Siberian wastes , even on Pisgah's slopes ... dotting the hills of Europe, the lands of France and Spain ... pausing, to mark, at Morbihan, the passing of the years in Carnak's stones ... reaching the utmost confines of the Western Sea ... only to find ... *no isthmus* to the longed-for land.

Their dead alone they launched at Cap de Raz, praying that heaven-sent winds might waft *them* to the "Islands of the Blest."

(These ancient stories were the Scriptures of the Druid cult, which cult we know lingered in the remoter parts of Wales even in the seventeenth century!)

Then, as man learnt how to build better ships, he tried again to bridge the barrier which had so long divided him from his old home.

And the oft-sung Legend of the Druids crystallized to truth when Madog, son of Owan Gwynedd, a Prince of Gwallia, first sighted land in the Year of Our Lord 1170.

contents

illustrations

Dramatis Personae

MADOG, *Son of King Owain Gwynedd and Queen Brenda.*

OWAIN, *King of Gwynedd (North Wales) from 1137 to 1169.*

BRENDA, *Wife of Owain, daughter of Howel, Lord of Carno.*

CRISIANT, *A Lady of the Court, Owain's paramour, afterwards his wife; mother of Prince Davydd.*

PENDARAN, *A Bard, Madog's instructor; a secret devotee of the Druid faith.*

NURSE HUNYDD, *Foster-mother to Brenda of Carno.*

ANNESTA, *Madog's wife; a Maid of Honour to Crisiant.*

GWENLLIAN, *Only daughter of Madog and Annesta.*

MEVANOUI, *A friend of Annesta's*

HOWEL OF CARNO, *Brenda's Father.*

CADWALLON, *Madog's Chief Captain.*

DAVYDD, *by Crisiant; a Bard.*

HOWEL, *by Pyvog.*

CYNAN,

RHUN,

IORWERTH, } *Sons of Owain*

MAELGWYN,

RHODI,

FATHER JEVAN, *Priest of St. Gwifen's.*

GWALIOR, *The Court Chamberlain.*

MAXEM, *The King's Cupbearer.*

PECKÉ, *The Court Fool.*

FRATER PHILIPPUS, } *Knights Hospitallers*

FRATER ALBINUS,

book 1

chapter 1

the castle of aberffraw

THE champing of bits …

The clatter of iron-shod hoofs in the Castle yard.

The neighing of hungry steeds, who, nosing the sweet odour of home stables, whinnied to stalled companions.

The shouting of men-at-arms.

The braying horn for lagging hounds.

The yapping of thongéd stragglers.

… A whole bedlam of sounds claimed Owain of Gwynedd had returned from his hunting.

🎵 🎵 🎵

The Cupbearer issued from the chief door, bearing a horn of wine, which, lifting to his lips, Owain drained without drawing breath.

Then throwing the reins on his stallion's neck, he dismounted, and passed up the passage formed by obsequious courtiers, disappearing into the great hall, within which stood Gwalior, the High Chamberlain, bowing himself to the ground.

"How goes our royal spouse?" Inquired the King eagerly, "has aught happened since we left?"

"Sire, your lady is even now brought to bed of a son."

"'Tis good, 'tis good," he cried. "Maxem," beckoning to the Cupbearer, "another horn of wine." Which lifting high, his head thrown back, and all the muscles of his mighty neck outstanding, Owain Gwynedd drained, toasting his newborn son.

"Here's health to the babe, and damnation to his enemies. May his name linger on the lips of Welshmen as long as Welsh be spoken." Then handing back the empty horn to Maxem, and tossing his hunting knife and belt to a waiting page, Owain turned to his Chamberain —

"Can we yet see the Queen?"

"Yes, sire. She sleeps, they say, but if you would come noiselessly, she would not wake … and you could see your son. She prayed so earnestly, and made us promise e'er she slept, the babe should not be take from her chamber, and foolishly … I promised, knowing sire, that in your love for her you would not have her fever rise through fretting."

Down the great hall, along the stone-flagged corridors, the Prince followed Gwalior, till, reaching the portal of the Queen's chamber they paused, inquiring of the woman who opened, if "peradventure they might enter?" She beckoned assent.

Quietly the King strode in, his footsteps falling noiselessly upon thick skins that strewed the floor.

The Chamberlain, approaching the high bed, bent down, and listened. ... whispering —

"Yes, sire, she sleeps ... a blessed sleep, for it was mighty labour ... and her women feared she would not live her travail through."

Then, turning to the nurse—

"Woman, the King would see his son."

She lifts the babe, all bundled up in swaddling clothes, from his mother's side, and hands him to the King.

"Undo the Prince, for I would see him in his naked person, whether he be well made ... and strong and lusty ... worthy to rule his fellow men ... for is he not my heir to wield the sceptre after I am gone ... to lead a warlike people against their foes ... and so he must be perfect."

"But, sire," pleaded the nurse, hesitating, "he is but this same instant washed and clothed, and he would be enrheumed to death were I to strip him now again!"

"Woman, unrobe the babe."

Slowly, with trembling fingers, and many pauses, Hunydd unfastens the wrappings, till in her lap lies a red morsel of humanity, struggling and straining. The King touches it, and turns it over ... and then ... as if suddenly arrested, looking intently at the left foot … then at his Chamberlain.

"Gwalior?" he questions, "this is a malformation? Owain's sons have never 'fore been crippled. … He is of no use to me![1] His foot is clubbed, and lame and limping all his days will he be going. … It never shall be said that Gwynedd's seed is impotent! Take him away at once—and when the Queen awakes, good Hunydd, tell her the child was weak and breathed its last whilst she was sleeping. … Women forget these things in time, and she shall have another twice as fair."

A feeble cry came from the bed—a woman's sobbing.

"Owain, Owain," moaned the voice. He walked towards her and taking the frail hand held out, stooped down and kissed it, and, pressing his lips to the forehead where beads of anguished sweat were bursting forth—

"Dear one," he whispered.

"Owain, Owain," came again the piteous craving cry. "I heard, I heard. … Your will is my commandment. But, oh, grant me but *one* boon"—she paused exhausted—"that … that … before he die, he may be purged from all his sins by holy baptism … and I … shall pass content."

The King pondered a moment, as if dissatisfied and half inclined to deny her wish, hesitated again … then, shrinking from her eyes —

---

1. According to the Welsh laws, any disfigurement barred a Welsh Prince from reigning.

"It shall be as you ask," he bent nearer to her. "O my beloved, why has Heaven sent us this great trial? Many sons have I, yes, great strong lads, and I had hoped through you ... whom I adore ... to have created one as beautiful as Christ Himself. But—my brave chiefs must never know you bore by me a cripple, such as *this*"—he pointed sadly to the whimpering child. "Sweet Brenda, give not way to foolish tears, I would not lose you also, dear ... You must be brave, and soon you will be well again ... and then ... " —he pressed his lips to hers—"the blessed saints will send you sons ... you shall be proud to name ... not useless hobblers." Seeing how weak she was, he took her hand, murmuring, "Your wish is granted, wife," and, kissing, left her.

"Gwalior," he turned angrily to his Chamberlain when they were out of ear-shot, "you said the Queen was sleeping. Curst luck that she should hear ... but can't be helped—send you a priest and let her have her way ... an then to-night —or in the early dawn —creep in and carry off the child, and drown him in the moat—perchance he may himself be dead by then through too much baptism, he looks a weakling babe, more fit for brat of priest than son of king."

"Hunydd ... Hunydd." It was the voice of the Queen, calling for her old nurse, "Hunydd dear! ... O woman of Ceirinion, O foster-mother of mine infancy, can you remember when I held your breasts? Can you yet dream of pink-tipped fingers mouching your warm skin? Hunydd ... Hunydd. ... *You* cannot give him up! my babe! and tear from me all you once loved so fondly? ... Hunydd ... you will not ... will you?"

She paused, seeking strength to continue. "Dost remember, as how I grew, you tended me ... guided my feet ... and taught my tongue to frame that name, so dear! ... 'Hunydd,' such a sweet name? Do you not love me still ... my foster-dam? Mother," she whinnied, "you will not let them take the babe from me ... Hist, woman! bend me down your ear!"

Brenda began to whisper feverishly, although her lips were trembling so that she could scarcely frame the words; her eyes shone with a light so fierce —- yet tender —that they looked like living flames amidst the deathly whiteness of her face.

"Hunydd," she was saying, "you must take him away to Ceirinion ... the live child ... my live son ... I will give you gold and jewels ... and all your days you shall be rich ... and happy, for having given joy to one who loved you so" —pausing—"for having saved a Prince." ... She broke off utterly exhausted, then, after a long pause, began again in a low voice: "You must go down amongst the poor at eve, to the turf hovels near the Castle gates ... so many babes are born, and die, in those dark holes ... and find me one ... and when the King sends for my Son to-night, thus shall you say, 'Alas! He is already dead,' and wrapped and bound in all his swaddling clothes, they will not stop to look for a club foot." Then Brenda, falling back amongst her pillows, lay there, whiter far than they, breathing as one in pain, trembling from head to foot.

That night at sundown came priest, with all his servers and his acolytes, and entered the quiet chamber of the Queen.

In solemn pomp, Owain offered his son to God ... for life. Wrapped in a cloth of gold, entoured with all magnificence of princely state, they named him "Madog."

Then when the mists had risen on the sea, and blotted out the sand dunes and the bay —when dust had spread her cloak across the hills, Hunydd went tramping through the mud midst squalid huts, and found at last a dying child, and gave the hungry mother bits of gold, and took the stiffening corpse within her shawl. Returned by a back entrance, climbed up the scullions' stair, where none would challenger her; washed it, and wrapping it in linen, lightly bound it, feet and all; and in its rags she placed the Prince, returning the hovel—adjured the weeping wrench to keep him safe till three suns rose and set, when she would come to fetch and carry him away. And, sworn upon the cross to secrecy, the woman took the child.

🎵 🎵 🎵

At early dawn, when all the world was grey and cold and hopeless, the Chamberlain crept in, and woke the sleeping nurse.

"I have come," said he; "is the Prince ready?"

"Oh, sir!" said the woman, sobbing bitterly, "O sir, after his baptism, the child was taken with convulsions, and died within the hour, 'tis no necessity for murder … for he has gone beyond the pale of human reach … so sure the sign of Him the Crucified was marked upon his brow, he went to join the children of his Lord in Paradise … see there he sleeps, and I, worn out with sorrow, slept beside his cot."

🎵 🎵 🎵

Three days had passed, and Owain Gwynedd, who had gone again to hunt the boar in the woods round Snowdon, never guessed that his wife's old foster-mother, Hunydd, mounted upon a pack, had ridden through the Castle gates, escorted by two stalwart knaves, armed *cap-à-pie*,[2] bear-

---

2. From head to foot

ing a burden in her arms, "a gift of munificence from the Queen," she vowed, from which would not part, "for fear of robbers!"

Strange treasure! That wanted nourishment whenever halt was made!

Six days they rode, till she reached Carno in Ceirinion, her own old home, where Howel ap Jenaf, the Queen's father, was the over-lord, Prince of Arystli styled.

Then, very stiff and sorry, and muchly shook about, Hunydd dismounted at her brother's door, and showed him all her treasure, gold and jewels, and coloured linen stuffs … and last of all … mannikin … he asked no. questions, and she told no lies! Thus Madog rode to Carno.

🎵 🎵 🎵

Five blessed years she loved and tended him, and then came death, and warned her she must go.

But Hunydd—before she passed—sent message unto Howel, and prayed him come and see her e'er she died … and he being present …

"O, my lord Howel, five years ago, your daughter, the Queen Brenda … as you know … gave a son birth. They called him Madog … who being halt, the King his father would have slain, but, by connivance, she and I together saved this same child's life, and he … is here to-day … the

11

sturdy boy, who plays on yonder green, should call you 'Grandsire.' But I must leave him ... for One has called me home, therefore I cannot stay to tend him here. But far away in Môn lives an old Bard, Pendaran by name, wiser than living man, and kind. My Brenda loved him much, and would that he should guide her son upon the road that leads to wisdom, and I pray you ... 'tis Brenda's wish ... when I am gone beyond my baby's calling—he may be sent to him."

And Howel ap Jenaf, who honoured much his daughter's nurse, swore upon his sword's hilt that he would send the boy, with trusty escort ... for he, too, had heard of Pendaran's fame (for was it not spread through the width and length of Wales), and knew that Brenda's choice was good.

The summer heat was passing fast, and autumn fogs spread early cross the vales, transforming even flying rooks to whiteness of the gulls; the dripping leaves clanked sharply in the moisture-laden air—as Hunydd—crooning softly "Nunc Dimittis," between fierce spells of pain, slipped quietly out of life, to pass beyond the boundaries of the world ... and Madog ... coming to sup, could not awake his Nanny ... and would not eat his bite, but sobbed himself to sleep, a-calling "Hunydd."

chapter 11

love-in-a-mist

ALL day the Queen had ridden a-hawking, with marvellous good sport, but as the evening drew to a close, she found herself divided from her ladies, and on a track she did not know—and worse still, a sea-mist rising, promised every moment to blot out the surrounding landscape—even now the hill peaks appeared as islands in an ocean of white fog, and soon she realized, as her palfrey stumbled down the stony bridle path, she could not see horse's length in front of her. 'Twas a chilling mist which enveloped her, like some ghastly pall, shutting her out from earth, world and humanity.

She shivered, as she endeavoured to keep her palfrey on his feet; 'twas no nice prospect, forsooth, a night upon the mountains. Of course, when the Court reached Llaneilian, where they were housed, and found she was not with them, they would send to search for her ... but still, that might not be for hours … an meanwhile it was lonely … and … there were wolves … not many … now perhaps, but still some few. … Through the mist she conjured up shadowy forms, dodging in and out between the rocks, and keeping pace with her.

A sudden rustle in the bracken at her feet made her horse shy … and she cry out in fear … but it was only a human form that met her startled gaze, a boy … a small brown boy, the kiss of the sun on his tanned cheeks, the rime of the fog glistening his hair; his half-clothed limbs were strong and straight and beautiful only he waled a little lame! From his face shone big and wondering eyes!

"Little lad," said the Queen in Welsh, "can you tell me where I am? An which is the track to the Monastery by Eilian's Shrine?"

"You are on Trysylwin Mountain. I do not know the way to Eilian's holt, but Pendaran does—he travels much about, and sings at monasteries and courts; some day," he continued proudly, "when I can sing quite well, I too shall go with him, and he will take me to the Court at Aberrffraw, to see the King and Queen."

"Is Pendaran's home near here, my boy?"

"Oh yes; if you will follow me I'll take you to his cave, 'tis hardly fifty paces off."

"Good little lad, the saints will bless you; but I thought Pendaran lived all alone!"

"Oh, not now, lady; *I* have lived with him since harvest time, a whole month now … ever since … ever since" … the boy's voice broke into a sob.

"Ever since when, my man?" The Queen laid a kind hand upon the thick dark curls.

"Forgive me … lady…" Still he sobbed, then with an effort, choking back his sorrow, "Since Hunydd died. O Hunydd, Hunydd," wailed the home-sick child, big tears running down his cheeks.

"And who was Hunydd, bâchen?[3] Oh say, she is not dead!" A sudden thought bursting upon her.

"She was my nurse, my Nanny, I lived with her at Carno; and then one day, when I came home to sup, she lay all stiff and white, and would not answer when I called her … and when I kissed her, did not kiss me back … and then came Howel ap Jenaf, the great lord, and with him twenty men … he mounted me, and bade them bring me here … so far … so far away from Carno. Pendaran is kind … but I want Hunydd, Hunydd," still he sobbed.

"Your name is Madog?" The Queen's lips trembled as she framed the name. The blood had left her face, her heart stood still.

"It is, good lady, but who told you so? I am five, but I shall be a man some day, so Pendaran says, if I eat oaten

---

3. Little one

bread … and I can shoot as straight as Owain Meredyth, and he is twelve … and I can swim as far as Caradoc … but not run quite so fast as Llwyd … because my foot is hurt, but none can see I limp unless I run!"

What was stirring all her pulses, making the blood surge so wildly through her veins. … What was this mad exultant joy? The mist that had seemed but a moment before a pall entombing her in death, had now become a heaven-sent cloud, wrapping this child and her in a golden haze of happiness, blotting out the dead world beyond.

His brown eyes looked trustfully up to hers, as he babbled on, reciting all his prowess … this noble little lad, who five long years ago, had nestled for an hour within her breast. And he—he wondered why this grand lady on the horse should look at him so fervently. Even as they talked, they emerged upon a grassy plateau, at one end of which was visible a cave; and at the entrance, shading his eyes with his hand—as though endeavouring to pierce the ever-thickening mist—stood an old man, tall and erect, with iron-grey hair brushed high from off his forehead. His clearcut features, and piercing eye, giving him resemblance to an eagle. He was wearing a leathern jerkin and short hose, for he had been digging in his garden, his garden of herbs and simples. (For this instructor of men, this singer of songs, Pendaran, the Druid Bard, honoured labour as man's highest sphere, his *raison d'être*.) Here he lived, summer and winter, high in his eerie nest on Trysylwin Mountain, except at such times as he donned his robes, and visited Aberffraw, or other courts, where for his learning and for his melody he was ever welcome. Or to hold amongst the mainland heights, Gorseddaw, for the enrolling of new Druids. For though the Cross was preached through Wales 500 years, many of the Cymrii still clung to the old faith, and the power of the Druids was far reaching, their councils often influencing the princes more deeply than the outwardly accepted advice of semi-Norman priests, who took their *queue* from the English Court, or Rome.

When he had recovered from his first surprise at seeing Madog accompanying a horsewoman, he came forth courteously to greet them. Then bowing as he recognized the Queen—

"My good Pendaran," she said, as he helped her to dismount, "a blessed home it is to me this night, for I had lost my way, and feared my home would be the mountainside, with wolves for bed-fellows, if I had not met yonder little lad. Oh Pendaran … tell me, it *is* he, it *is* Madog, is it not?"

"yes, lady, Madog it is; just four weeks pas he came, bringing a letter from your father, begging me to keep and teach him what a boy should know, saying you had expressed a wish, when he was born, that some day I should be his pedagogue. I knew that some time you and he must meet, but never dreamed so soon." Then beckoning the boy, who was gazing open-mouthed, "Come hither, this good lady wishes to kiss you now ... stay! You are all stained with berry juice. O Mochen!"[4] But the Queen would not be denied, she caught the tumbled youth against her heart, and stained him to her breast.

Oh, the warm fever of that first embrace, sending the hot blood whirling to her head.

"Ah, Heaven! ... at last ... at last" ... she held her son, her treasure, her great joy.

"Madog, Madog," she whispered passionately, she could not think ... only feel, lost in elisian.

For an hour or more she sat thus, questioning him, learning all his baby thoughts, and hopes and sorrows.

Suddenly, the braying of a horn woke up her mist-enshrouded world ... from peak to peak it echoed ... then again ... heavier this time.. shattering her joy ... she drew the child to her again, kissed him with a lingering fervour ... for now she could see, plunging up the track over the ringing stones, a steaming charger, and on his back Davydd, Owain's son by Crisiant, who as he reached her...

"My Lady Queen, the Court is in an uproar! We feared that you were lost!"

"So I was, Davydd, and should be now, but that this stripling found me wandering, and brought me into

---

4. Mochen: little pig.

Pendaran's cave, who was preparing even now to guide me back to our guest house at Eilian's Shrine, but I will come with you, good Davydd." And kissing Madog once again with lingering wistfulness, Brenda remounted her palfrey, and passed into the mist, that hid from her a new-found heaven. Yet as she rode, and listened to her escort's chatter, a childish voice seemed calling her, from far away, and she, as one that dreamed, enshrined within a maze of golden love … marred only the bitter past that sprang to mock her, the remembrance of the years marked by the gradual cooling of Owain's love for her, till now … till now! the hot passion had grown cold and dead.

What did a warrior want with childless wife! Childless!! could he but see this beauteous boy with eyes of mother-love! Forgetting for a moment that impediment in moving. Must men be ever thus, gazing alone at herculean frame, voluptuous contour!

"O, Maodg, Madog," she sighed involuntarily, as an echo of a childish voice floated down through the mists from the hill above.

"You are not listening, Queen," grumbled Davydd, "and the joke is really fine; think of Pecké, dear droll Pecké, with the immaculate Dame Vargam on his knee!" he roared enormously at the idea, and the Queen politely laughed in unison.

"But why immaculate? Who is this Dame Vargam?"

"Oh, don't you know? the tale is worth repeating for very quaintness! Oho! Oho! the saints are wise, their keepers too do learn the trade with short apprenticeship, and soon can earn their profits.—A little shrine—a wonderworking saint—is worth a mint of gold, when skilfully manipulated! … Well, returning to our dame! Sad fate, that baulked of other loves, brings poor old Vargam to set her cap to tinkle jester's bells! 'Twas al St. Dwynwen's[5] fault, of course, of course she bears the blame!! Full twenty years ago, within her sensuous shrine kneels Vargam (the rich yeoman's only child) praying, prostrate before the Celtic Amphrotrite, a-pleading hard for love … there meets the young Lord Iorwerth, a-seeking something new…. He likes her looks, and offers what she seeks … and soon the tower of her fair virtue is pulled down … and e'er the passing of a moon, the enamoured wench falls in her gallant's arms …

5. St. Dwynwen, daughter of Brychan Urth, a holy man, lived in the fifth century. She was the British Venus, or tutelary saint of lovers, and her votaries were very numerous. This patroness of amatorial connexions was profusely supplied with offerings, by sighing nymphs and rejected swains. The bard of BROGININ thus addresses the sea-born goddess. "Dwynwen, fair as the hoary tears of morning, they golden image in its choir, illumined with waxen torches, well knows how to heal the pains of yonder cross-grained mortals. A wight that watches within thy choir, blest is his happy labour, thou splendid beauty! with afflictions or with tortured mind shall none return from Llanddwyn." An Abbey was founded upon the site of her shrine (the ruins if which still stand upon a sandy peninsula southeast of Newborough). So wealthy was her treasury at the time of Owain Glyndwr, that it became the subject of a serious depredatory quarrel. According to the visitation made in the reign of Henry VIII, the revenues constituted one of the richest prebends belonging to the Cathedral of Bangor.—*From Evans' N. Wales*

St. Dwynwen smiles!! Then coming to herself, she knows her shame, but the home door is shut; … she robbed her of her mind, for twenty years poor Vargam's mind was blank! Then came a day, a year ago, when she walked back to life … and knew, and felt, as you and I to-day.. but twenty years were blank, and still she thinks she is but seventeen, though she be forty nigh! Ha! ha! he! he! poor damozel, poor damozel!—a-looking into Coron's lake one windless morn, beheld a buxom dame, with quarters like a cow, and hair turned grey, and puffing 'neath her eyes … and yet … a heart … a heart where beat the passion of a girl. St. Dwynwen smiled no longer at her devotee … until she sang! and the hermit, who served his Venus night and day—perceived our Vargam's power, and promised her fair love, if she would chaunt at matins and at evensong, to his assembled supplicants (those who enriched his chapel with their gifts). Discerning man, that priest," remarked Davydd, with a splutter …

"And so she sings, pours forth the passion of a maiden's breast before the shrine of Heaven! Whilst others drink the nectar that her words evoke; streams of celestial passion prodigally cast before these herds of men, who hear and are turned mad—a solemn sacrifice to Love—ambrosial flood whence her own dry lips may never more draw sustenance. Oh, Brenda, 'tis a woeful tale, alas, so quaint, I roar in thinking on it … a young girl's heart embedded in that fifteen stone of flesh! a music of the gods evolved from out an old dame's maw! A mouth that stooped to touch a Pecké's lips! Ha! ha! ha! ha! O queer, cruel irony of years."

"Ah, Davydd," said the Queen, as she turned in her saddle, to watch him holding his sides with the laughter that promised to split them. "Ah, Davydd! How oft a woman would change places with a hermit crab, that she might choose her shell to fit her soul … but so it is to-day, the envelope that covers many a heart is like an oyster clinging round a pearl … man looks, and sees a thousand grey green shells, but may not guess within which shell the pearl is laid … thus—oh, Vargam, poor and old, beneath your mound of flesh a soul is hid, a shining soul—thank God, that you have found one vent for its sweet fragrance, betraying through an angel's voice those depths of throbbing pain, wherewith to salve some other human hearts, and touch and comfort them; wafting them echoes of the melodies of Heaven, though you yourself must suffer in dread torturings."

Brenda paused, her pitiful eyes wet with tears…

"But oh! the piteous shame of Pecké's kiss … the sin … that Love should cover with his name the breath of God, and lewdest appetites." There was silence, neither spoke for some time, riding on through the night—this youth of seventeen and Brenda of Carno, his father's wife. At last the flare of the braziers that burnt around the royal camp lightened the heaven, and soon they were within the guest house of St. Eilian's, which place was in an uproar at the mysterious absence of the Queen, and only quieted down when her safe return was noised abroad.

chapter III

"jealousy"

CRISIANT sat thinking in her closet, within the Castle of Aberffraw, the logs were burning merrily on the open hearth, and autumn sunshine filled the room. Crisiant was in the habit of thinking, her brain was very active; she knew all that was going on about the Court; to her came those wishing to find favour with the King; to her came those who had some poignant scandal to retail, some much cairned secret to disclose. Half the chiefs were in her pay, either by money … or by kisses! —all the servitors! She rewarded handsomely, and it was bad to be her enemy, wise to be her friend. Once upon a time Owain had made great love to her, and Davydd was the pledge … then he met Brenda and made her *Queen*! Crisiant did not forgive…

Five years ago Owain adored his wife … but now … through judicious interferences—unintended constructions thrown upon her actions … drops of poison here … drops

of poison there, much profit made of childlessness …
tales, half-true, and wholly damming, whispered insinu-
ations … Crisiant had won the day … Owain no longer
loved his wife.

But yesterday, a messenger had arrived from St. Eilian's,
where the Queen had so soon gone again hawking, and
he brought news of import, for he had seen her palfrey
tethered upon the grassy plateau near Pendaran's cave,
had watched and seen the Queen come out, and then had
gathered from a swineherd on the spot, that whenever the
Court was hunting in the neighbourhood, the Queen rode
there, and sat with old Pendaran for hours.

"The crust old Druid," muttered Crisiant between her
teeth. "Now why was Brenda there? … Could it be possible
that she was at heart attached to the old Pagan Creed, that
Pendaran priested?" She must watch her closely, quietly,
not to let her guess. She had wondered why the Queen had
gone a-hawking so oft of late, never had she sown much
love for sport before. Well, if her visits to St. Eilian's led
so often past Pendaran's cave, 'twas very sure, (whether
the truth or no) that soon the King might be persuaded to
believe she favoured Druidism. Oh, she knew wondrous
tales, and might improve upon them … of human sacrifice!
of children sawn in twain … or burnt with fire. … Why not
discover some poor churl's babe, and swear the Queen kid-
napped it for her heathen rites! …

She chuckled at the thought, holding out her white fingers to the blaze, till she could see the warm blood glisten through the skin. Rubbing them together as she purred her great content, picturing the triumph of her ingenuity. What a blest dispensation of Providence it was, her spy should run the Queen to such a pregnant ground. She laughed soft and merrily as she wove the warp to catch so old an enemy; not the King only, but all the Court would hound the heathen woman from its midst. … Ah, all the thousand pains the Church let loose on cursed heretics, who differed from her holy creed, should sear the form of one her lord had dared to love—such tortures! Crisiant laughed again; she could almost fancy the scent of burning flesh came from the fire—such tortures! and then, a stake piled up with faggots belching tongues of flame, a foretaste of eternal fires!

♬ ♬ ♬

"My lady," it was Margaret, who disrobing the Queen, before attending her to her couch. "My lady, when you were at the cave to-day, a man passed by, and from his face I guessed he'd seen your palfrey, and wondered why 'twas there, he had the appearances of some watching wight or spy. Princess Crisiant has her paid men everywhere, maybe she overlooketh you with hope of scandal for your master's ear, and will invent some escapade of love, say you were even seen within some gallant's arms! Believe me, you must not go there again to see the boy." Brenda half promised, but with the dawn had changed her mind again, and rode in the direction of Trysylwin Hill, and reached the cave before high noon that day—also the next, and next, and next; and Crisiant was not uninformed.

For six months the Queen was happy. Owain was away upon the borders, fighting the ever-encroaching English.

Then came the night when he returned, weary with war—and drinking deeply, drank not over wise.

And after supper, when Brenda had retired, he sent his Chamberlain to her closet, to ask if he could speak with her; and she returned a gracious message, welcoming him.

Then when he came, and they were both alone—he towering in all the majesty of his great height—his brow as black as thunder, his fierce eyes ablaze with hate, he turned to her. ...

"Queen Brenda, will you tell me why you go to Eilian's Llan so often now to hawk—and hawk alone—for bats, in Pendaran's cave? What fascination has old age for you? Unless,"—he caught her by both wrists—"unless you work with him the works of hell, and offer sacrifice to his curst gods. Answer me, witch, if your black tongue cleaves not within your lying mouth to-night."

Never a word uttered the Queen … she stood as marble … speechless … motionless.

Owain looked her sternly up and down … ah, it was hard to believe these hands would stoop to wrench the life-blood from a babe! … but Crisiant had had the cave watched diligently, no mad had made it a trysitting place, and none lived there except a dotard and a child.

"Brenda," the King came close to her, his hot breath fanned her face, "I loved you once," he sighed involuntarily, "I believed in you, I trusted you; you have betrayed that trust. Yet … for the love that burned me long ago, I will not press you now … but … if again you venture near the Druid's cave … a stake, a pile of faggots, burning brands … and Brenda's ashes shall be winnowed by the wind. Now, wretched woman, I can understand why holy Bridget[6] withheld her blessings from you, why God sent nothing but a crippled child … it was His curse upon an unbeliever."

The King paused, then with stern, relentless face, he turned to go … he walked across the reed-spread floor … closing the great door behind him … leaving naught but deadly silence in his wake.

---

6. Bridget, the patron saint of births.

The woman heard the echoing footsteps passing down the corridor … then all was quiet again.

She threw herself upon her knees beside the open casement … her life had been so happy these few months, the wound of Owain's neglect had been new salved by this great love she found within her son, and now, he too was wrenched from out of her arms.

"O, Madog, Madog," she moaned, but there was none to hear, save the great sea heaving in the moonlight without, breaking itself against the rocks that had repulsed its impetuosity, so she too seemed to break herself against a stony world that wanted none of her, and the waves of love she offered but recoiled—sobbing, to her own heart!

But even as her eyes rested on the silver waters of the bay, the sense of her loneliness seemed lifted; as from the surrounding "fron,"[7] there rose a melody of voices of the past, the great ones who had inhabited this place, who had lived and suffered here for centuries past, St. Gwifen, in his lonely little cell, amongst a host of pagan savages—the great Howel Ddà, and many priests and kings, and 'twas not the undying names alone that hallowed hill and wake, but the passing of innumerable feet who came to venerate the dead, and looked with wistful eyes longing towards the ragged Snowdon range. Those undeveloped souls who

---

7. Fron: slope

tried to soar above the scented flowers, and larks that sang in the blue welkin. A myriad unsatisfied longings seemed to haunt the sobbing wind that swept this unknown world, of which she formed so small a part. Oh, the soft calm night that lays her mantle over all, quieting the crying of her human babes!

"O, Madog, Madog, love brought thee life, and now thy love would bring black death to me."

So Crisiant triumphed yet again, although she guessed not 'twas a mother's heart she mangled in her snare ... but smiled next day to mark the pallor of the Queen.

chapter iv

"a link of the past"

INE after line of white breakers rolled in over the stretch of wet sand, spreading and losing themselves with monotonous roar, ere curling back with baffled sob to re-inforce the waves behind.

The storm was over now, but it had been terrific while it lasted, and Nature, like a passionate child, though hushed, could not be quieted all at once—still a thunder echoed from the waves, a moan escaped the wind, as the angry leaden billows heaved restlessly up and down. But the shrieking of the furious gale, was now a whimper ... the storm-god spent with fury, could but whine and grumble ere he sank to rest.

A man and boy were walking along the shore, turning over, here and there, the damp sea-wrack washed up, for on this dangerous coast there was no telling after a tempest what guerdon the waves might have brought.

"Madog," said the elder man, pausing when they had gone the length of the fore-shore, and were making towards the land, "to-night I will tell thee the secret of my life," he hesitated—like a man about to tear out his own heart—the muscles of his face contracted with the strain. His eyes were turned away, gazing across the sea—turned away from the lad, into whose hands he was about to tender all his hope, all his ambition, his talisman of life.... "I am an old man now," he paused, "at last the bitter truth is forced upon me, the day has come ... when my dim orbs can never more be lifted to the Star of HOPE ... others must accomplish the task of my beginning through my enfeebled fingers the thread of destiny is slipping ... my day is passed ... and I ... must leave to younger men the accomplishment of all I held most dear ... Madog," he laid his hand upon the boy's shoulder, his burning graze now fixed hungrily upon him, "Madog, you are still a youth, but older in the head than years ... I—knowing not when death may claim me ... give up to you the knowledge which will make the world ring with your fame ... the quest is yours, where I have failed ... failed after half a hundred years of fruitless scheming." He paused again, his face grey and hard in the waning light. The young man waited. Above, the sea-birds were being whirled against their wills by feckless winds ... beneath, the whines and rushes clacked together in the salt sea-breeze, that blew the sand about their feet; then nerving himself as with an effort, the Bard began...

"Long ages ago, the cradle of mankind lay in the west, but a great deluge came, and drowned half the universe, only some few being saved in one large ship ... so say our legend ... to which ship drifting on and on for days and months and years, the flood at last abated, it rested on the mountains of the East ... in Bactiana, now so called, and from the hulk of his great bark, crept out some half-starved creatures of the human race, and wallowed in the mud coating the solid ground, dear Mother Earth, which they had never dreamed to see again. Then catching stranded fish and digging roots, slowly regained some strength, and then amidst the caverns in the heights, they found some famished beasts, in direr plight than they themselves. But soon the world began to breathe again, and as the years went on, the green grass sprouted where the slime had been, and slow, but sure, the waters shrank away, and man and woman mated with their kind, till growing numerous again they spread, and wandered with their herds. And one great tribe, the sons of Japheth, your own ancestors, with homing instincts made towards the west, from whence they knew they came, pausing in one land first, and then another one. So generations passed, and nations rose and fell; awhile they bode in Chaldee, directed by their priests the Magi, who looking in the face of heaven, read the stars for help. But ever wandering offshoots left the parent tree, with longings westward-bound, until they reached the sea and crossed to Defroban, now Constantinople called, and there some stayed … but later generations swept across the face of Europe, and ever on towards the setting sun … till they arrived in Spain and found the dry land ended there; they paused, and called it Celtica … and then crossing the Cantabrian hills some men went north to Gaul, but found no further isthmus there, seeing but ocean spread unending to the west. Here many paused, and counted years by stones, until in Morbihan[8] they'd raised a wood of holy monoliths, which stand in silent proof to-day, the oldness of our face … others meanwhile made boats and tried the sea, but sailing many days could find no trace of land. But some few tempting round the coast, beheld a northern isle, crossing the narrow strip Mortawch,[9] landed in Britain and soon possessed the place … and laid their mighty Temple to the Sun, Gwaith Emrys,[10] which still stands, as it has stood 2,000 years. In peace they lived, their Druids, Fathers, Priests and Kings, custodians of the wisdom of their world, a wisdom treasured (but kept secret, not for vulgar ear to learn) … thus knowing much, guided and nursed their tribes, directing all their doings—providing

---

8. Morbihan, at Carnak.

9. Mortawch: the German Ocean.

10. Gwaith Emrys: Stonehedge.

laws; —yet, ever yearning towards the west, in hope of message from their cradle land, but no sign ever came. But though no living passed, they sent their dead, and launched them from the Bay of Souls, at Cap de Raz in Brittany— even to-day—when with a sigh, the spirit frees itself from bond of clay, they push their little navires from the shore, bearing their holy freight, that peradventure they in death may sail the intervening seas and reach the land from whence their forebears came. Ah, Madog—here, in Wales, the Cross has stamped out old beliefs … only a few remain who care for ancient lore … but firmly I hold faith that when I die, I shall pass westward, though on no mortal ship, as I had hoped to do. Ah, in these Christian time 'tis all forgot, that regions ever lay towards the west, but, Madog, *it is true*," a look of triumphant certainty illumined the old man's countenance, "true as that we once owned Britain, north and south, and east, till barbarous hordes came to its shores, and slew our ancestors, and would have stamped our people out, only we flew to Cambria's hills, or to Hibernia's bogs or Highland fastness. Here 'midst those mountains we have lived for generations past, till came the monks and lured away our flock, preaching a beggar Jew, cursing our holy rites as heathen cult, till just a few were left who held the ancient faith our fathers handed down. Oh, deaf and sightless followers of Christ, to whom the trees are voiceless. Ye see no spirit in the hill, or goddess in the stream; ye cull no future from the changing stars, nor bow in adoration to the orb of day. Ye have forgot the histories of the past, dimly remembering, that ere Nöe crossed the sea ye dwelt within some blessed paradise, ye've never sought for since!" The passionate timbre of his voice was heavy with scorn. "*We* know, *we* know, the happy land from whence we came, know the same land still lieth there." He pointed to where a watery streak of sunset yet remained.

"O, Madog, that … *that* land has been the loadstar of my life, to reach *that* land again.. but fate has willed it otherwise." A sigh of hopeless renunciation escaped his lips; then taking both the boy's hands in his own…. "All this I learned when I was yet a youth, graduating for the Oveyddiate,[11] this legend of our race, which every Druid knows. They say that 'tis a wondrous land, with palaces and temples, and that its men are lithe and strong, of swarthy hide, brave in the chase, and furious in war. But, since man first carved the record of his acts in stone, no echoes of this world have crossed the seas. Yet oft at night I've dreamed about this land, till such a longing gripped me, Madog, I could think of nothing else!" He sighed, "I often asked if there were proof of this old story, but only answer came 'The Druids never lie.' Then a great resolution formed itself, grew bound

---

11. Oveyddiate: lowest order of Druids.

within my heart! some day to know, some day—before my feet descended to the grave, to sail across those leagues of sea for many dawns, towards the west, that peradventure I might reach Elisian fields, or die in the attempt. Then," here Pendaran paused, passing his hand slowly down his white beard.

"Then ... 'twas such a night as this, on the west coast of Erin, where I had gone with my father on embassage from the Prince of Gwynedd. I was walking along another storm-strewn beach, when my attention was diverted by what seemed to be the carcase of a tree; carelessly—as curious youth will ever do—I turned it over, and saw, not tree, but hollowed out canoe,[12] and in it tightly strapped with thongs of hide, a human form, with noble face—all strained and drawn in death—but finely chiselled featured, high moulded brow, and straight black hair, swarthy of tint ... and on his wrists, which lay against his sides, two golden bands or armlets, yes, one on either arm, dimmed by the sea ... but strangely graven ... and I! I stood transfixed! a thousand thoughts were tearing through my brain. ... THIS THIS! from whence? ... was it some nightmare dream, and should I wake or ... was this shrivelled form a message from the other world!"

---

12. In 1893, a long canoe, made from a dug-out mahogany tree, was washed ashore off the Needles, and is supposed to have drifted from the shores of the West Indian Islands.

For a few minutes the old man neither spoke nor moved, as if enacting all the scene again. Then he continued—

"Scurrying clouds were blown across the moon—the bitter night-wind whisked the sea-wrack in my face, and howled amongst the pine-trees on the cliff … but I could not tear myself away … for hours I stood unmoving … thinking … thinking … thinking … until at last I saw the lighting of the dawn. Then having fixed my mind I cut the thongs which bound the dead man to his boat; lifting the stiffened body in my arms, I bore it—gently as I could— unto the upper sands, where sea-spray never came, and then I scooped a shallow grave, but ere I placed him in, I slipped the golden bands off his wrists … and here," the old man bared his shrunken arms, "here they have rested till to-day … and many times, at many courts, where I have craved a ship, and cruel disappointment had night heart-broken me, I've looked at these, until new hope was born … but now, crueller than kings or potentates, courtiers or courtezans … comes Death, or his forerunner *Age*, and when Age comes, then Hope is lost, and naught remains. Hope is the sap of life, which running dry…" He bowed his head, and stretched his gaunt hands out to the winds. The boy did not speak or move, his grief seemed too sacred … then at last raising his head, "Madog, these armlets, I loose them now—to-night, from off mine arms … to place on yours … for some day … when you shall learn your birth, and claim your birthright, may demand a fleet—to do your bidding—for you ... when you are a man, shall sail across these very seas ... which my dim eyes may never now behold!" ... Tears—impotent tears, rolled down the old man's cheek; but neither spoke again until they had regained the cave.

From that night onwards Madog seemed to have grown older; there was a new bond, a holy secret between him and his instructor; he listened with greater earnestness to the teaching of the Druid, he asked more questions, he learnt more readily the legends of his race, the songs of war, the songs of love and praise, than he had ever done before.

He was now fourteen, and had not Pendaran promised him that when he was sixteen he should accompany him to Aberffraw to sing before the Court! ... only two years ahead and still so much to learn!

Together they worked, the old man slowly giving up his grip of life, the young man surely gaining his.

Yet Pendaran was happy, he saw himself again in the growing boy ... through him, he thought once more the thoughts of youth; he drank once more the fullness of the spring! And then the day would come when he should see this lithe, strong stripling's brow encircled with the "Baridc

Crown," for so it would be, of that his soul was certain. Never was blood-father prouder of his son, than Pendaran was of Madog.

Quietly the years rolled by; what time Madog was not studying he spent in his fisherman's coracle on the rough waters of Caernarvon Bay, or the rushing floods of Menai Strait. Never was youth happier than he, fighting the elements, tossed by a raging sea, from mountain wave to deepest watery vale.

Something within him answered the sea-bird's cries, shouted exultant to the screaming wind! It seemed to lift him from the mundane ways of men, and carry him aloft to some wild glorious life that he had lived before, had lived before, and had not quite forgot. His being, all atuned to raging nature, nature, who too was striving hard to burst the fetters laid upon her unwilling half-tamed soul. Oh, the dull life on steady land—when one could plunge amidst the trackless waves at sea!—fitted perhaps for dotards and soft men—but not for burning youth! And he would scale the rocky cliffs for eggs, and catch the bloated puffin in its hold, or ride the fiery ponies on the hills; and ever kept the larder stocked with fish and game.

And so the years rolled on.

A short truce had been made with England, and the heralds rode forth the width and breath of Wales to proclaim a great Eisteddfod, which Howel ap Owain, one of the royal prices, was to hold for forty days at Aberffraw, calling the bards from far and wide to come and compete in verse, in melody and wit; with harp, with crwth,[13] and pipe.[14]

The morning of the great day at length arrived, and Madog, leading the hill pony on which old Pendaran sat, passed down the mountain-side at dawn. It was a good day's riding, from Tryslylwin hills to the far south of Môn. All day, through morning dew and midday heat they tramped, passing Tre'r-beirdd, through Christiolus Man— Trefdraeth—passed the three Court-houses[15] near to Corron Lake, until they viewed the towers of Aberffraw, standing out, above the clustering village huts, and glittering Ffraw. It seemed to Madog, when he saw them first, it was for this he had been waiting all his life.

---

13. Crwth: the original of the violin.

14. Pipe: Bag-pipes were rather popular in Wales in the twelfth century.

15. Court-houses: Hen-llys-fawr—Hen-llys-wen—Hen-llys-croes.

Mother and son knelt thus embraced, the secrets of their lives revealed.

chapter v

"a queen's lover"

IT was evening—the din and clatter of the banquet resounded on every side of the great hall of Aberffraw. Soon noon-tide, song had followed song, poem chased poem through the hours. Odes to the King's greatness, his warlike exploits; the castles burnt, the neighbouring princes slain, successful raids against the ever hated English bands. All were enumerated, every bloody deed of the past year extolled.

Then Pendaran rising with his harp, sang the high praise of Aberffraw, of its great strength and beauty, the splendour of its halls, the largess of its lord—the spreading Vron, all carpeted with flowers, the fish that sported in its bay, the corn it grew, its fragrant trefoil fields....

Brenda, who listened, felt a mist of bitter tears was rising to her eyes, as memory re-awakened, pictured a long past other day ... when bathed in autumn sunshine, she had first ridden, in sight of these grey walls which topped the earthworks … how stately then to her they had appeared, with their rough masonry, after her father's spade-dug Castell in the south. This great palace, which was to be her home … the woman sighed … her home! … 'twas but a prison now, and the lord? her lord—her jailor … and Crisiant the torturer … Crisiant who worked the rack both night and day.

Brenda turned to where they sat … the King flushed with much wine, his left hand stroking the golden veil of his paramour's bright hair—whilst she leant in voluptuous abandonment against his shoulder, her blue eyes gazing amorously into his.

None seemed to wonder, every man was happy with his own fair dame, his own horn of wine. War time was hard and dure, but peace brought love and luxury. Another minstrel was singing now … Pendaran had finished.

At first she could not distinguish either words or melody, the laughter of half-tipsy warriors, the squeals of bantering women filled the air, but at last the hubbub began to subside a little.

What song was this … surely familiar? …

Bright are the leaves of the ash as they glisten,
Touched by the moonlight shaft. Oh, my love, listen!
Sweet is the breath of furze, breathed on the summer night,

Bidding thee, tenderly, pander to my delight;
Hear'st thou the corncrake chaunt, song of his mating?
Fragrant the clover bank, why art thou waiting?
Come, oh my love, to me, bring me thy gladness,
Heaven lifts her vault for thee—blessing our madness.

It rose to the groined roof, and echoed across the hall, it hushed the ribald jests of the drinkers, this wild passionate cry of the lover, a-calling his loved one.

Ah ... now ... she recognized it ... an old song she used to hear in her girlhood's home ... a song which ever sent the blood a-tingling through her veins.

Then she had wondered when one would come to cry thus for her ... and prayed the saints it might be soon.

Ah! they had heard her prayers. Owain had come riding across the hills, had come ... and sung thus to her ... and she ... she had answered to his singing, giving heart to him and ... but who was this singer? this youth with the exquisite voice ... who made her pulses throb again ... as they had not throbbed this many a year, and whence had he learned this song, that she had never heard since Carno days? None were likely to know it here, except perhaps old Pendaran, who travelled all the country-side in search of melody.

Then ... as she listened a sudden thought made her heart stand still ... had Pendaran brought this youth? Who was he?

Long ago he had told her … ten years ago, it must be now, "Some day Madog shall sing to thee."

It could not be Madog, and yet … and yet! The she remembered the warning.

"When Madog comes, beware! for none must guess, none know, only thyself … *hide well thine emotion!*"

Slowly the pallor of the Queen gave way to scarlet, the blood was mounting her head, her fingers tightened on the lion masks of her chair, the hall seemed growing dark, everything to be turning round … the company was wrapt in mist.… She only heard a ringing voice vibrating the hushed air.

Come, oh my soul, to me, bring me thy gladness
Heaven lifts her vault for thee, blessing our madness!

Her heart seemed opening like a thirsty flower, craving that madness, that wild, strong madness. Oh, this passionate cadence, awakening the old longing of youth, the old yearning for love! Then the revulsion came, leaving her parched and sapless, with no further hope of life than to drag through years of weary existence! The last words died away; followed by a thunder of applause.

But Brenda sank back into her chair, covering her face with her hands, but none noticed her; hot tears were rolling down her cheeks, wild thoughts of what might have been, were chasing through her brain.

She saw the crown of oak-leaves being placed upon the young minstrel's head, her eyes sought his, and he, he was looking at her, seeking her approbation … and as their glances met, she knew, she *knew* that it was Madog!

Later in the evening, she sent one of her ladies to Pendaran, and bade him, when the feast should be finished, to bring his pupil to her apartment, so that she might hear him sing again.

At last the revellings were over, Crisiant had supported her smiling lord to his couch, and many slept beneath the tables, where they had fallen.

Queen Brenda rose, and attended by her ladies retired to her own chamber, and thither presently, Pendaran brought Madog.

Then again within the walls, where so long had silence reigned (save for the murmur of unanswered prayers, or bitter sighing of an unloved wife) rang out the songs of joy, and youth and gladness.

Queen Brenda slept that night like a young girl dreaming old dreams of sunshine, birds and flowers.

And Madog, tossing on his bed of fern—where he lay beside Pendaran in the distant guest-chamber—wondered why the Queen had looked so kindly on him!

A week of feasting, melody and verse, went happily by; and every evening after meat, when all had gone to rest, the Queen would send for Madog to sing to her.

But there was one whose eyes were ever searching damnation for Owain's wife, one whose sharp tongue was ever lapping poison to spit Owain's ears!

"My lord," murmured fair Crisiant, as sitting on his knee, she stroked the King's rough cheek. "My own dear lord, think you not that Brenda grows more beautiful these days! The music of the bards makes her of cheerful countenance, and when that young bard sings, the one who won the oaken crown the opening night, she looks as though some heaven fenced her round; seems it not strange that the sad Queen, who scorns your love, should throw her wanton glances to such beggar minstrel lads? Noticed you not, my lord?"

The King had noticed nothing.

"Then watch to-night ... when Madog sings ... the old bard's *protégé* ... a handsome youth, well-made ... with fawn-like eyes ... such as a woman loves ... think not because the Queen is cold to you, her heart is dead. But watch, my lord, I would not fill your mind with evil thoughts, where no cause is."

That night, when Madog, sang, Crisiant nudged the sleepy King, and Owain blinked his eyes and watched.

Brenda, who had sat listening with vacant stare till then, sat up, and all the sinews of her form seemed strained ...

her face was very pale, but the great eyes glowed with a hidden fire, and her lips moved, as though she too would sing ... she saw nothing but the youth, heard nothing but his voice.

Crisiant spoke to her, but she did not answer.

The King stretched out his staff to touch her, but she did not move.

"Am I mistaken?" queried Crisiant.

The gleam in Owain's sodden eyes grew cruel and fierce.

"The boy must go," he muttered with an oath.

"No, not before you see if there is guilt ... each night, I hear he visitest the Queen, and sits with her, and sings to her, almost to matin time. Be not too hasty, lord, see them for yourself. To-night when we have been abed, let us arise, and pass along the secret corridor which leads unto the chamber of the Queen and see ... what we shall see!"

The King swore sullenly beneath his breath and early went to bed.

'Twas midnight. The guard was being changed upon the battlements. The Castle lay hushed in silence, save for the clanging of those metalled feet.

In the Queen's chamber alone rang the notes of a harp and the clear, strong voice of a young man. Madog, standing as he swept the strings, his brown hair thrown back from his forehead, his eyes gazing far away, for he was singing of the country of his dreams, the land beyond the sun-down, and Brenda sat and listened, as one entranced. When he had finished she questioned him about this country of which she had never heard … and he … he poured his hopes and longings into her sympathetic ears, and prayed her that some day she would use her influence, to get for him a ship, that he might in surety try to prove the tale of Druid lore.

For long they talked … and then he, with flushed face, showed her the armlets … his holy talisman … which none had ever seen before … she touched them with her hands…

Conversing thus in happy confidence, he looking round the room, admiring the rich hangings, espied in a far corner an oaken cradle, and over it a canopy, whereon embroidered in fine golden thread were worked the letters of his name, his own name "Madog," and waxing bold with curiosity, asked the Queen if she had ever had a child? as he had always heard her called "The childless!"

"Ah, madam, sans doubt, I had a mother, but never has her name been spoken to me, and never her lips pressed mine, but my old nurse, my own dear Hunydd, used to sing sometimes the songs she said were hers—ah, they are beautiful as breath of spring, yet full of sadness, as the wet rain swishing through the rushes after autumn storm; shall I sing one of them to you?"

And Madog sang.

And as he sang—the tapestried walls around melted away for Brenda. She felt the first faint breeze of dawn—she saw the cobwebs quivering with dew, hanging like diamond threads upon the cotton grass—she heard the plaintive call pee-wit—pee-wee—the clap of circling plover wings … the mad wild singing of the lark, rising to meet the sun. Beneath her feet the springy moss of turbary … within her heart beat thoughts … passionate and wistful … of waking womanhood.

Then Brenda, Queen of Cymrii, bent her down until her arms were laid upon the frame of the tapestry—her needle halted in … her whole being rent with sobs … as the fair past arose again to mock her with its sweet.

Madog, alarmed, threw himself at her feet, cursing his vain folly, which had Brough suffering to one he passionately loved, kissing the hem of her white robe, begged her forgiveness … and she … the Queen, placed both her arms about his neck, and drew him to her, until her warm lips met his trembling ones.

"Madog," she said very slowly, "Madog, was my son's name, Madog is yours, there is only one Madog, you are he." The words were whispered…

A great silence fell upon the room … her ladies, who had been in and out till within the last few minutes, had gone to prepare her couch. Mother and son knelt thus embraced, the secrets of their lives revealed … and heart was beating against heart.

Then—in a moment, a portière opposite was madly torn aside, disclosing Crisiant holding back the enfuriated King. In his hand was gyretting a long spear, which before a word could be spoken, sped like a flash of lightning through the air, crashed into the tapestry frame and buried itself in the rushes on the floor, passing within an inch of Madog's head.

The youth sprang up, stood for a moment irresolute.

"Go," whispered Brenda—an open casement was behind him, she pointed towards it. "Quick!" He sped across the floor, leaped on to it and disappeared.

A sudden splash, then all was quiet. A groan escaped the woman. Then slowly rising, pale and defiant, she faced the maddened King.

He, striding across the room, stood towering over her.

"Whore?" He hissed through his clenched teeth, bringing down his hand upon the work-frame, smashing it into a thousand splinters—"Whore? Is it because I gave you no son that you must call this half-fledged wastrel to you? because you beget not man by man, you would conceive zannies by a whelp like this. *Lâche*! who treats me with such coldness, that I am driven to find love in Crisiant, this is the game you play … a thousand devils take him … how often has he kissed you, wanton?" and catching her by the shoulders, he shook her as he would a dog.

"Owain, you lie, and you know it." The pale Queen was drawn up to her full height, commanding in her nobleness. "Call my women, they have never left the chamber, they are but in their own compartments;[16] behind the arras, never for one moment have we two been really alone. Nesta," the Queen calls out, "Margaret, Gwenlian!"

With scared looks the Queen's ladies emerged from behind their curtains.

"No, sire," said Margaret, "we have not been absent, but passed each moment through the hall, and listened to the singing of the boy; he could not speak two words without our hearing, we sat around whilst he played many songs, but it was growing late, and we prepared the couching of the Queen, and put away our trinkets, and just when he was going, you came in."

"Oh, Satan take the lot of you, you're the *lâches* all with lovers hidden in your lairs. God curse the Queen, and every woman like her in the land." And turning on his heel, he passed with Crisiant behind the arras, down the secret stair, of which he held the key.

---

16. Beds were curtained off round the room, much as cubicles are to-day.

What little sunshine had shone in Brenda's heart was now extinguished. Owain refused even to speak to his wife, except in public. Pendaran was forbidden the Court.

She had heard the dull thud of the boy's body falling into the moat, but since that time no word of Madog had reached her, and she knew not whether he was dead, or if he had escaped.

The dull days dragged on. Owain left again for the Marches. Then in the autumn the harvest failed, the cry of famine rose from off the land … the wail of starving men and women pierced even the Castle wall. She denied herself almost everything to help them, but still the nights were horrible with those who howled for food. She herself felt sick, and something seemed to warn her, her day was passing fast … for love and hope alone nourish the future, and without them, we were already dead!

She dared not acknowledge Madog as her son, for she knew the day the truth were even guessed would be his last … if still he lived! Better let the King believe him lover than the crippled heir of Gwynedd. Owain was brave, but he was cruel; assassination to him was but an everyday occurrence, and those that stood in his way were soon put out of it.

Slowly faded the beauty of the Queen, so thin, so white she had become, appearing but the shadow of her former self, that Crisiant laughed with glee, her blue eyes bright with unwonted mirthfulness; her day must soon come now, when she should rule as Queen, and not as mistress only; then her son Davydd should be legitimized—her brave, her comely son—who ever fought for his great father in his wars, and led his hosts. For Crisiant ever plotted, that when Owain should be dead, Davydd should take his place.

Margaret, the Queen's lady, was fretted much about her health, and sent for herbalists, who with wise looks and many questionings, pronounced "a marshy fever made her sick," brewed stews of simples, seasoned with eagle's heart, and badger's gall … but all had none effect. All day the Queen would lie upon a couch beside the casement, whence Madog had leapt out. Far away, across the sand-dunes, and the bay and land beyond, she could see the Caernarvon hills, and her thoughts would travel back to her father's home, her father whom she had not seen since the time she rode away a bride.

Messengers had brought news of him from time to time. "Truth, he was growing old," they said, "but able still to lead his forces in the field."

Crisiant visited her often—ostensibly to care for her and cheer her, retailing the gay doings of the Court, but deftly insinuating that things went merrier far now she was absent, hardly able to drive back the triumphant smile that rose so readily, as day by day she saw her rival weaken.

The months passed on and winter came, and went—Owain was yet away engaged in border raids. Though it was spring the cold was still intense, causing much suffering to the poor, but Brenda cared not now, the outer world seemed passed from her, of no account, no longer listening to her ladies' talk or songs. Spring merged to summer, June was come. Still she lay there, although insensible. Then one grey morn near sunrise, she oped her eyes and looked out upon the sea, she seemed to hear a voice approaching her across the floods, surely 'twas Madog's voice borne up upon the breeze, then it rang louder, louder … then, seemed the fluttering of many wings, raising a hurricane … till something stretched to tension seemed to break; a mighty convulsion, a quivering … the soul of Brenda, Queen of Gwynedd, passed.

Owain was still away, keeping Henry of England off his borders.

Crisiant, arranging for fresh festivities at Aberffraw, had risen early, it was she (so kindly sympathetic?) who, coming to ask how Brenda had slept, started to see the figure on the couch was reft of life … a mocking laugh ruffled the chamber of the dead.… She had no rival now!

"Brenda," she whispered, bending down, "the fool who crosses swords with me must rue her folly; poor weakly dolt, who truckled to a man instead of driving him, deprived of son, despoiled of mate! Sad saint … so ends a wasted life." She would have spat on the dead face, but shrugging her soft shoulders, "Waste of good spittle!" she jeered.

Then calling Brenda's ladies—who slept late, after a night of watchfulness, retired to her own apartment, whence summoning the Chamberlain, she spread the news, and bid him send a messenger to Owain, who bivouacked at Rhudlan; and ordered fit preparation for the funeral of a Queen!

chapter vi

"the hospice of st. john de carno"

THERE was a drowsy hum of summer insects ladening the air of the Refectory, in which Madog sat, vainly endeavouring to keep awake and fix his attention upon the illuminated manuscript that lay on the desk before him.

The scent of the newly-mown grass of the "Corphlan"[17] was borne in at the casement, whilst from the chapel beyond came the monotonous chant of the Brothers.

In Madog's brain, sleep was mixing up metaphors … bedizened saints were treading measure with dancing gnats, and he wondered if it were sunshine, or the glow of frizzling heretics that fanned his cheeks, facts and fancies were becoming a hopeless tangle, when suddenly the clatter of a galloping horse woke the sleepy lad to mid-summer existence.

---

17. "Corphlan": land surrounding a church.

It was seven months now since Madog had dropped from Benda's casement into the Castle moat, and swam across, thus escaping the fury of Owain; but still fearing capture he fled to Carno, where there was "Sanctuary";[18] Sanctuary where even the vengeance of kings was powerless. All the winter he had been kindly entertained by the good Hospitallers, who took pride in instructing this young heathen in the cult of Christ … and he … he endeavoured to entrance himself with the ecstatic lives of saints, who ever sought new paths to Heaven … half amused … half sympathetic—divided betwixt admiration for the holy simplicity of their Faith, and the wondrous extravagance of their believings!

The clanging of iron-shod hoofs ceased at the chapel door, and Madog saw a man and horse covered with dust and sweat pull up; one of the Brothers come out hastily, a few whispered words and he disappeared into the cool darkness of the church again, to return with Howel ap Jenaf, who had been there confessing.

For a long time Howel and the man held conversation, then Howel, perceiving Madog, walked across the grass to the open lattice where he sat, his face drawn with suppressed suffering, the tears standing in his eyes.

---

18. "Sanctuary": "Whoever shall take sanctuary, may walk about within the churchyard and the burial ground, with relics upon him."—Laws of Howel Dda, A.D. 928

"Madog," he said, as the youth stood up to greet him, "the Queen your mother is dead." Then he told the boy of all that the messenger had informed him. How three days ago, after months of sickness, they had found the Queen with her sightless eyes gazing eastwards.

Jenaf was very fond of this grandson of his, whom after an absence of twelve years, he now had much with him.

Madog listened to all he had to say, but it was not till the old man had ridden away that he began to realize all that it meant to him, realize the frustration of what he had been hoping for, the meeting again with his mother; for wild schemes had entered his mind of entering the Castle in disguise, some time when Owain should be away, and holding her once again to his heart—and bitterly now he mused upon the impassableness of the door death closes behind him, as he escorts his chosen across the threshold of his own domains. He saw in imagination once more the scene of that first night at Aberffraw, Pendaran bidding him to rise and sing … ah, how he had trembled—how his hand had shaken, as he nervously fingered the strings—what a lump had risen to his throat as he endeavoured to articulate the first few words! … till … as he continued … the hall, the courtiers, even Owain himself seemed to recede, and the sad face of the Queen stand out alone, that pensive face, on which sorrow and patience had mirrored a sacred beauty, all its own … that face whence the magnetic eyes cried to him in their love-hunger, drawing out his very soul … till … he was singing to her, to her only … and she … she was his mother … and now … his head sank on the missal, his whole frame shaken with sobs…. Ah, he should never see her more … never feel her mother-kiss, her warm breath upon his neck…. Hot tears followed each other down his cheeks.

"O God of Christians," he moaned, "hast Thou a Kingdom where the dead may meet!" This—prostrate with grief, Brother Albinus found him, when he returned from stabling the messenger's horse.

Madog stayed on another month with the good Hospitallers, but now, all hope of re-visiting Aberffraw was gone, he began to find the monotonous regularity of saintly living somewhat irksome.

The Hospice was a dependency of the greater house of Halston; the six Brothers who formed the community were vowed:—to befriend the poor, receive travellers and convey them through the dangerous passes, which stretched north and south, east and west through Carno, which village was the central point of Wales.

These passes were infested with robbers, bands of dangerous marauders, who killed and plundered all such as ventured without strong escort through their hill defiles.

The Hospitallers had rebuilt the church, to which already belonged the privilege of Sanctuary; they had done what they could to instruct the half-savage inhabitants of this mountain country, and instil into them some rudiments of Christian morality.

Madog liked the spirited brushes with the banditti, the exciting rides along the valleys behind the rocks of which crafty cut-throats might be lurking, but these excursions were not of every day occurrence, and he began to tire of lauds and matins, exortic saints and holy contemplation!

He began again to yearn for the old sea-life, for freedom and adventure. He formed an ardent wish to go to London and from thence take ship to distant lands, of which he had so often heard. At last he divulged his thoughts, and begged the good Brothers to further his designs, and let him go.

And they, recognizing the impatience of youth, forth-with made arrangements for his journey, giving him recommendation to the Knights of St John at Clerkenwell.

So Madog went … and stayed with them … and saw the sights of London town, and when he had well seen, took ship and sailed from Thames to Mediterranean; and there he spent three years, trading from one port to another—from Venice to Phoenicia—from Orihuela to Mahadia, from Alexandria to Genoa, and learning what he might of navigation and astronomy; hearing strange tales of many lands, of beasts and birds and savages, his curiosity being ever fired by all he heard to greater zeal. And all furthered his belief in the old Druid legend, that kingdoms ever lay beyond the vista of known continents, and strengthened his determination, by hook or crook to get ships and test the truth of his believing. So after three years of voyaging he returned to London. One thing was certain, he was now twenty-two, and must begin to realize his aim. Long he pondered over the almost unsurmountable difficulties that rose before him; no help could come from England, though he now spoke with fluency the English tongue; the Plantagenet King had too good cause to hate his countrymen, who sorely plagued him, ever to help in any enterprise mooted by man from Wales! He could get no sympathy in London, he must return to Gwynedd, and see if he could not obtain perhaps some influence at Aberffraw, through Jenaf, who had now made treaty with Owain.

But first he would go to Carno and learn how things were faring up in Mon.

🎵 🎵 🎵

A month later ... Brother Albinus a-working in the garden, heard the clanging of the postern bell, and, as was his custom, went to welcome the traveller, whomsoever it should be and give him blessing.

"You've come from far, good friend? 'Tis sultry weather for a horse to-day; bad luck that brought you here a Friday too, but still the Carno trout are fat, and I caught one this morn that turned the scale at 3 lbs. 10 and such a fighter! such a fighter! When I had landed him—and stood upon the bank to thank Our Lady he broke me not—I shook and trembled like an aspen!"

"Brother," broke in Madog laughing, "am I so changed?"

"Holy Saints! 'tis our young heathen! indeed, indeed, you've altered much, great hulking man," taking him by the shoulders and peering into his face, "but now I see your eyes—I know you, Madog, and we are glad to have you back again," he continued, embracing him. "Come haste, 'tis near to supper time." And thus talking garrulously he led him off to dust him down.

Soon the stains of travel were removed and Madog sat amongst the Hospitallers in the Refectory once more. There all remained unchanged, it might have been the very night that last he supped! three years ago—yet over him a whole decade seemed passed.

He looked through the Norman arches towards the little Chapel of St. John beyond, darkly silhouetted against the steep Clorin's side, which lay bathed in a glow of rosy light!

"Benedicte," came the deep voice of Albinus.

"Edent pauperes, et salurabuntur; et laudabunt Dominum, qui requiremt eum vivent corda corum in soeculum soeculi Gloria," echoed the answer.

"Kyrie eleison" … "Christe eleison … Kyrie eleison."

The "Pater noster."

"Ad coenam vitae oeternoe per ducat nos Rex eaterna gloria."

"Amen."

Alternatively rising and descending, the grace before meat mellowed the air, till the echoes died away.

"Here's to your good health, son Madog," and the Brethren stood and drank to the new-comer … a clatter of empty tankards, a sigh of satisfaction….

"Now tell us how you like the world," continued Albinus, "and if it's half as marvellous as you dreamed? Have you been yet to Holy Land?"

"I landed once at Jappa, and stayed me there three weeks. But I have seen enough of Soldiers of the Cross, to stain with gore the whole of Palestine." Then with a twinkle, "Although I'd warrant more ruddy wine would ooze from them than blood!"

"Ah, Madog, Madog, ever hard on Christianity, your unregenerate soul can never comprehend the beauties of our Faith."

"O yes, I comprehend, dear Brother, well enough, but fail to see the point. Within a land, a thousand leagues across the sea, you strive to wrest a sepulchre where no man lies (for if He lay there now, then all your faith were void!)."

"Unreasonable, ever unreasonable, dear lad, do you not realize that country where Our Saviour"—crossing himself—"where Our Saviour lived and taught is trodden by the heathen infidel, and every spot defiled, which He had sanctified!"

"And will you make it purer by washing it with many nations' blood?"

"We do but shed our blood for Him who died for us," chimed in Philippus, with uplifted eyes.

"And what good will it do to Him? O Brother, Brother, forgive my heresy, but the longer I do live and voyage, the stranger seems the myth to me, that one man's blood, one God-man's blood (spilled now ten centuries ago) is payment for each sin you do to-day; no, no, Philippus, man's recompense for good and evil lies within himself … a good life spent will bring him to a world of bliss beyond the grave, or evil down to Infuriun,[19] to recommence the fight. But I will speak no more," seeing the hurt expression of their faces, "of that which wounds the souls of such true men; forgive me, Brothers, that I so did blab … but, all in haste I do withdraw my argument, and humbly crave your pardons. 'Tis simple want of faith that makes me heathen; if I had faith, I too would lay me down at night and sleep the blessed sleep of shriven man, knowing my sins washed white, my pass to Heaven sure."

"God give you grace, and some day bring you to the Fold," said Albinus, raising a hand in benediction.

---

19. Infurin: the purgatory of Druidism.

"Amen," chaunted the Brothers. For a few minutes there was silence in the Refectory.

"I thank you for your kind forgiveness, sirs," said Madog, annoyed with himself for his late want of tact. "I journeyed not to Carno to preach heresy, but to see old friends again, and also to crave your aid … in just the same old matter which really took me hence."

"Ha, Madog! still crying for the moon, and yapping after lands which don't exist?"

"Exactly so, Philippus, my old beliefs have hardened since I left. I have not told you yet, that when at Sais, I met an ancient Scribe, who recounted much strange tales, I scarce could credit him. He said … long centuries ago, before the days of Noë, his nation lived upon a land beyond the seas, far to the west, that during an upheaval of the world, many were crushed or drowned, but some escaped in boats to Africa, and settled on the Nile … and from old papyrii, taken from the tombs of kings (those of most ancient dynasties), he believes that part of the submerged continent still exists to-day, and I feel sure 'tis the same land of which Pendaran's legend speaks, that which the Druids ever knew, for they (our Celtic ancestors) in times gone by, had traffic much with Pharaoh's land" … Madog paused convincingly.

"Tut, lad, a man can dream, and piece and dovetail, till fancies fit as fact. If such a land had been, would Moses not have told us of its being! But if such land there were, how would *you* find it?"

"Good Brothers, I have come to Carno even now to ask your aid in this great enterprise. I wish to go to Aberffraw, to beg from Owain such a fleet, that I may sail across these endless seas, and seek for what I *know* is there … or die in the attempt," said Madog, pressing gold circles of the armlets into his flesh to give him further confidence.

"To Owain's Court, are you quite mad?"

"No one would know me now, Albinus, changed so from boy to man, from white to bronze, from thin to thick, from treble voice to bass, smooth cheek to raven beard!"…

"Dear friend, go no to that wolf's den again. Great King, brave soldier Owain is, but Wales groans 'neath his cruelty. Pauses he to take a life that harries him? He thinks you dead, and thus he wishes you. Should Brenda's whilom love be recognized!" the old man shrugged his shoulders, "a little poison in your mead…. Own up as Howel's grandson! he wants no crippled whelps to claim his blood! … Ride there as adventurer begging a fleet!" Philippus held his side and roared until the rafters rang, "to beg so small a gift as twenty ships … you'd spend one evening as the Court buffoon, the next as carrion for his hounds! Ha! ha! he! he!" chuckled the much-amused Hospitaller.

"Give me but chance, and let me try my wit; my life is less to me than mine ambition. I'll go as Howel's new minstrel, whom you recommend? Deft with the harp, and quick at the pennillion, with voice of flowing beauty!" here Madog cleared his throat and winked! "You have not heard me yet, Ah! many a woman's heart has stopped ... then beat with quickened madness ... when under warmer suns I sung to her! for, Brothers, blood runs faster in the south, as well you know. Say now, do Welsh hearts never yearn in sprint-tide for brown circling arms, and great eyes melting into theirs?"

Albinus coughed.

"Jesu Maria! hold, Madog, hold! don't us break our vows; we've all got our hearts and blood, and eyes ... and lips ... which wished to drink from other lips!" he sighed involuntarily, then crossed himself ... and filling up his horn with mead, washed down the sacrilege.

"To Madog! King of the Western World!" he drank laughingly. "Old friend, we will do what we can to help you in this quest ... this mad adventure ... for mad it is, God knows! and you are going to your grave ... perhaps at Aberffraw ... if not, beyond the confines of this world.... But let's make cheer to-night; sing to us, Madog, with 'that voice of flowing beauty!'" he guffawed, "but not too hot, dear lad ... about our sisters' lips."

Gently the songs began, but as the night wore on his singing grew more passionate ... he watched the casting of the faces as he sang ... for some waned sensual, others full of tears … many had loved, and music re-awoke their memories. And then, at couching-time when all was done, Philippus retiring to his cell, reached down a missal, full of women saints, and kissed their praying mouths, and thought of Dwynwen's chapelry … Albinus with his burning heart, took out his scourge and scourge his flesh till matin-time.

A week passed by, and all was settled now; Howel had been interviewed, and learning the whole truth, and wishing to do what he could for his dear Brenda's son, promised to send message unto Owain (who after much fighting now had become his over-lord!) to say, "He wished to please the Prince of Gwynedd—and hearing he was sick—sent unto him his favourite Bard, to cheer him in his hours of pain. One Doag, whose sweet melody would still the direst agony. A comely man, of noble lineage."

So Madog rode to Aberffraw, at Howel's recommendation.

chapter vii

the coming of love

ALL things were greatly changed at Aberffraw. Owain had married Crisiant, without the sanction of the Roman Church—she being his kinswoman. Thus for long years the Court had rested under the ban of excommunication, to which the King had been indifferent in his days of health, but now that death seemed menacing him, and manly powers had declined, he grew more fearsome at the thoughts of hell and coveted a pass to Heaven.

So he had humbly sued the great Becket for pardon for his sin, and was again received within the shelter of the Fold, and re-endued with pious thought and deed— endowing many churches and retreats, and doing penance for his graceless past.

Doag (as Madog now called himself) was made much welcome when it was found his music allayed the humours of the King. No one seemed to recognize Queen Brenda's whilom lover, not even Crisiant, though he felt her eyes were ever watching him.

He spoke nothing of his project, but endeavoured to ingratiate himself with all about the place.

Then—when all things promised fair—he was overwhelmed by circumstance, quite unforeseen.

A new element entered his life, and for a space he was swept off his feet, by that great torrent which uproots mankind, submerging all at our time or another, that stemless tidal wave—named Love.

At one side of the eastern battlement, rises a tower, known as the Dovecote; here were housed the many pigeons, used by the garrison for food. To the terrace surrounding this tower, Madog would mount every morning, to compose new songs, and practise on his harp; it was a quiet spot, remote from the busier parts of the Castle; here he could sing to his heart's content—his voice disturbing none—borne away by the winds across the green island, or wafted downward to the sea beneath.

One day—some five weeks after he had come to Aberffraw—he climbed to his familiar haunt, and sat dreaming beneath the shadow of a buttress; presently he became aware that he was not alone, a voice was calling … a woman's voice … followed by the fluttering of innumerable wings … then exultant coos of gladsome recognition.

Approaching through the morning mist, he saw a girl ... the silver light of dawn illuminating her face ... her fair young figure ... draped in blue, was silhouetted against the grey tower. Now, she was holding up her arms to the pigeons ... calling them again, and they came fluttering down, perching upon her neck and arms, circling around her ere they lit.... She lifted the basket of the grain she had brought as an offering to the winged multitude, and they fell to eating hungrily, no jot afraid. It was a gladsome sight, this being of divine beauty, half girl, half woman, standing thus, amidst the beating of a thousand wings!

Madog's heart throbbed furiously.... She emptied her basket of the grain, then turned to go ... but in so doing her gaze was attracted to his ... she looked up, their eyes met.

Madog felt the blood rush to his face as she started and turned to go.

"Forgive me," he stammered rising, "I did not mean to frighten you, do you come often here?"

"Yes, every day," she said, "but I've been laid aside these six weeks past, and have not left my room," with a sigh of remembered *ennui*.

"I thought I had not seen you at the Court.:"

"No, I have had long holiday. I am Annesta, one of the Queen's ladies, but the hot summer brought a fever, and I've been a-bed four weeks at least, but now am mended, praised be Our Lady." She paused, crossing herself.

"And you come every day to feed the birds?"

"Yes, every day at dawn. Crisiant rises late, and I am free till nine. It is so beauteous here at dawn, the wind blows freshly from the sea, the sun shines brighter too than down below, and then my birds … Oh, how I love my birds … the flutter of their wings … their myriad wings around, seem echoes from another worlds … till my heart beats … beats till it fain would break the fetters of this flesh … and I be free to soar to unknown heights of perfect ecstasy." For a moment she stood thus; her arms uplifted as though to reach the heaven of her dreams, her eyes, her blue grey eyes, like summer seas, grazing afar into her vision land—that Madog might not enter—"and they have nests … and little ones," she continued, "and they … they love each other so … and coo at mating time … *this* is my kingdom, all the greedy ones I punish by giving them no grain, and soon they learn, oh very soon; … they all have names, we are so happy here together," she continued smiling at the man; then her face fell. "But there are bitter days, dark days, when Andrew, the head scullion—hateful knave—crawls up at night, and bludgeons some … O Christ! the piteous wailings the next dawn, when mates are gone, and squeakers can't be found" … the great grey eyes filled with tears.

Madog held out his hand.

"Fret not, dear child, you still have many left … I too will love your birds, I also come at dawn, but not to feed, only to sing!"

"Are *you* the new Court minstrel Crisiant raves about? Will you not sing to me that I may judge?" She laughed provokingly.

"Not now, dear lady. I go to play to Owain, but if tomorrow you will meet me here, I'll sing you every ditty you can call!"

And thus they met ... and parted.

That night he saw Annesta waiting on the Queen, dressed in pure white, so young, so fragile, but with eyes all smiles for him.

♬ ♬ ♬

From that day onward ... come storm or shine, at sunrise near the Dovecote tower, a man and woman met, and as the days passed on, two hearts beat full together; two pairs of lips drank passion, each from each; two bodies felt the thrill of madding love; and whilst the pigeons cooed and mated, the lovers sat in silent ecstasy, lost in a dreamland of their own.

Below—far down below the hoary ramparts, the greensward rolled, and yellow sand-dunes stretched toward the sea, where grey brown headlands watched to break the surf; dim in the distance rose the mountain peaks of the Carnarvon coast. Up aloft they sat, these two, and watched the fishing boats glide outwards with the tide, following each other from the river to the sea. They listened to the life awake, within the Castle yard—the twitterings of the sparrows in the walls—the starlings with insistent chatter, scold and gibe—the swifts, whirl round with noisy screechings 'neath the battlements.

High, high above the mundane world … they dreamed … and wove a heaven of their own … there kissed and sighed— till love had forged the fetters death alone may break.

One day, when hoarfrost hung about the lazy dawn, filling the air with rime, and the first autumn chill sent long forgotten quickness through the blood, Annesta, emerging from the covered stairway to the terrace on which Madog stood—

"O Doag, are you here, you made me start! … I tremble so to-day … my limbs … which shake, obey not my bequest."

"Seren Siriol,"[20] he whispered, putting his arms about her waist (it was the name by which he ever called her now). "What dainty gave you nightmare yester-eve?"

"O Madog, was it nightmare? God grant it so, for such a dreadful dream I have not dreamed … I cannot tell you it … lips never frame what I have felt." She shuddered even as he held her closer.

20. "Seren Siriol": My bright star.

"Annesta, if you trust me not to-day, and tell me not your thoughts how may the years speed on when we are wed … you will not trust me *then* … a maiden's heart is hard to bare even to eyes which look on her as God … but 'tis this treasured, covered heart you promised me—I hold it sacred in my hands, untouched, and will not try by force to lift the veil, unfold the fairest thing on earth … but, darling—if you could but comprehend the pain to see through a dark veil, a jewel so rare, to know its radiance, oh, say for me, will you not uplift the veil, dear love, and let me gaze a little while … and cull the precious secrets there enthroned? … mine own, shall naked rise to yours … until our souls be wedded … each to each. One moment's Heaven is given unto man … in all his dreary march through life … the baring of *his* heart … and *hers*—on which no human eyes have ever gazed before."

"But, Doag," … she turned her away … for tears were welling up … this sacred shrine of her existence … no … 'twas impossible … her love was great, but still this something … this unplombed purity … this reigning God within … not even for him.…

"Then I shall know, I am no more to you than other men…" he walked away and stood apparently engrossed in examining a swallow's nest, built in an arrow slit.

Annesta, leaning her arms upon the parapet, burst into tears … he turned and crushed her in his arms.

"I am a brute … darling, forgive … I will not ask again … humbly I crave … I beg for your forgiveness." Closely he held her whilst she sobbed and sobbed … for some time silence reigned … then she, with a great gulp—

"Doag … Doag … I dreamt … I dreamt…" pause, "I was sitting by Llyn Coron, looking across its waters to the setting sun … which dyed the rippling surface gold and red, … and then, as there I sat … the shadows from the banks grew long, the swishing of the wind became less querulous … the fading glory of the sun leaving long shafts of glory, as he rolled away—beneath the world,—and o'er me crept a new wild feeling I never before, a sense awakening, yet uncomprehended, seemed stirring all my soul … I felt against my cheek something softly brushing … were words being whispered in my ear? or was it but the soughing of the wind … 'Annesta,' it seemed to say, 'listen—I will tell you what I am … listen and let your heart ache for such a one as I … for centuries have I been swept to and fro, o'er the sides of the mountain, wafted by every breeze that ruffles the face Llyn Coron … I have grown weary of being a will-o'-the-wisp, a zephyr … take me to thyself, give me new life … clothe me with flesh, let me become again a human being with throbbing heart, and thinking brain to feel again passionate touch of love!' 'O wandering soul,' I whispered, 'what wouldst you of me? how can I create for you this tangible home for humanity you desire?' … O Doag, must

I go on?" she whinnied; he pressed her hand, his face was deathly white.

"And in my dream, it whispered to me, 'Annesta, tonight, when the stars are like jewels in the welkin, the world wrapped in silence, the lake like a mirror, reflecting the vaulting celestial, wander out in the silence … kneel down in the hush of starlight … lift up your soul, pray, "O God, O Maker of all things, send me the love that createth, that I may give to this wandering spirit a home, a casement of flesh … a heart vibrating with life-blood, so that it, too, may feel all the love and the hope of existence."' Then in my dream … my eyes full of tears … my heart night to breaking, seeing the sun disappeared behind Holy Mountain,[21] the mist of the evening hand o'er the lake … like the breath on bright armour … the circles of rising trout had now ceased to ripple the water … the plovers had ended their day of sad calling … all the world lay a-hushed in a mantle of silence…. Then … as one by one out of the darkening heavens crept stars innumerable."

"Seren Siriol," whispered the man … he was not looking at her … he dared not…

"Then arising I dreamt, I stumbled through heather and bracken … hearing the sough of the night wind that rustled the fir-trees … was it the wind … or the sob of

---

21. Holy Mountain: Holyhead.

innumerable voices? crying out in their loneness. How my soul seemed to yearn, to take one to press to my bosom … blood of my blood … life of my life! Then I knelt down on the moss of the turbary … knelt … and raising my hands to the God, the Creator … prayed to be found worthy to be the home of some wanderer … prayed … till my whole soul seemed lift up and enshrined in a shaft of the moonbeams, and my being filled with ineffable happiness … the great orb behind Snowdon was climbing up high in its silvery splendour … long I knelt thus … entranced and exalted … till I beheld by its light, striding across the far marshland … O Doag … it was you … it was you, Doag…"

Annesta hid her face in the man's bosom and told not the rest of her dream.

☙ ☙ ☙

The summer waned, pushed roughly out by blustering autumn winds … but still they met, to cull the first fruits of the dawn.

☙ ☙ ☙

The winter hid the island 'neath his cloak of snow, and turned the sea to leaden grey.

♪ ♪ ♪

Spring came again with biting gales, and fitful sunshine hours.

♪ ♪ ♪

"O Doag," sighed Annesta one day, lifting a piteous little face to his to kiss, "if you *were* but a Christian, and would ask the Church to bless our union. I wake at night, dear love, and tremble when I think of your poor soul! I see you torn by devils, dragged about through hell! and when I fall asleep again, the screams of all the tortured ring within my ears … and *you* are gone—and some black demon whispers near to me, 'Never again, never again, shall your weak arms enfold him, for this your mate is Satan's child.'"

She laid her hand upon his shoulder, and cried wearily.

"O foolish little love, to feed on monkish legends. Why all your life made wretched fearing death? We are put here to live and love, and work and sing … I've lived and worked, and now," bending down and kissing her, "I'll love and sing, with you as guide start for my love and song. Oh beauteous is the earth where you have trod, the voices of the birds grow sweeter still as you pass by, even the flowers expand their leaves to catch the fragrance of your breath! Annesta, oh Annesta, it seems as if some exquisite cloud of love divine enshrines you, diffusing joy on all the air around! You are as far above the ladies of the Court, as mountain peaks above the valley rift, the sun of goodness touches and illumines you, whilst others lie within the shade, all cold and dull, reflecting not the beauty of its light! O my beloved, my beloved, why fret yourself with priestly tales? What place could Satan find for you? The very character of hell would change if *you* were there … and I … *I* fear not death and after, so long my course through life be honourable and straight." He took her in his arms and held her close to him, trying to dry her tears with kisses.

"Let's ask the kind old Lady Margaret to come to-day and wander through the woods, and I'll show you where the guardian spirits of the mountains live, and let you hear the larch gods sigh because they love the trees," he paused, "they love," he pressed her hand, and saw his passion reflected in her eyes, "they *love*," he repeated, his lips brushing hers, "and sigh to them, shaking the pollen and caressing pink-tipped buds, bringing fecundity from the other trees, extracting but their scent in payment … sweet pungent scent … which bearing o'er the fields they carry to our feet, to bathe us with their incense … and incense offered but to gods … we two are gods—because we love," he murmured with a long clinging kiss. "Annesta, all the world is moving, mating … for death alone stays love."

The dear old Lady Margaret, with a grey kerchief binding her white hair—loved dearly these young lives; her halting pulse throbbed again when she beheld their joy. "Yes, she would go with them," and through the quickening air of spring, full of the wine of life—they bent their way to the larch-woods near Llangadwalader and down to Gwna's stream; and she sat down, much wearied, on a boulder, thick with moss—took out her rosary, began to tell her beads … and think of other days … until the drowsy hum of insect life, the gurgling of the warming sun … the flickering alders, her mind … thus lulled, she fell asleep.

"Come, Annesta," pleaded Madog, stretching out his hand and catching hers, "and I will show you where the wild swans have built their nest, and if we both lie very still beside the otter holt, perhaps the cubs will venture out to play." And so they wandered on, their souls full of the mellowness of spring, until they reached the otter pool, and there lay down to bask.

"Can you not hear the spirit of the stream?" he said, "laughing as it rolls across the stones! then, as it nears the holt singing a deeper chant within the darksome caves. How bright the water paints the trees and flowers—reviving the parched meadows with its overflow and then … ah! 'tis a merry stream that rushes to the ocean, to lose itself within the sea-god's arms, and their offspring," he whispered, "'is drawn up into the heavens, descending on the waiting earth in rain! Ah, nature, always changing semblance, but ever renewing" … he drew her closer to him, and gathered her fast 'gainst his beating heart—she quivered.

"Annesta … An.. nesta … Annesta!" The Lady Margaret had dropped her beads in her slumbers, and was now on hands and knees looking for them … when the lovers rejoined her. "O my dears, where *have* you been? I've slept for hours, and my beads tumbled down.. and I cannot find them! my own precious rosary, blessed by à Becket." Then, when the evening air grew chill, and shadows lengthened on the grass, they crossed the sand-dunes back to Aberffraw.

chapter VIII

saint gwifen's shrine

"OAG," called Annesta, as she crept up through the breaking gloom to feed her birds, wrapped in a long mantle of furs, for the dawn was chill, even in May. "Doag," he came to her, put his arms about her, and laid his lips against hers.

"O love, I know you think me childish," she continued, "but I have come to ask you to beg Holy Church to bless our union…. I cannot live without this cementing of our bond." She laid her head upon his shoulder, the tears gathering in her eyes.

"Seren Siriol, if 'tis your wish, whatever you may wish is granted; we will go even now to Father Jevan, ah—'Marriages are made in Heaven,' but unrecognized on earth unless feed by Mother Church?" he queried smiling. "Come. before the sun is high, our union shall be ratified upon St. Gwifen's Altar." He took her hand and helped her down the stairway.

"But, Doag, I cannot leave the Castle before Crisiant's tiring time; she may have tear or tag for me to sew, but this afternoon, dear heart—and Mévanoui will come with me."

"Mévanoui? Why?"

"O Doag, forgive me, I have a dreadful revelation, for Mévanoui knows all. O love, I was so very lonely, and so very ill, and she was ever my best friend, and then she came and put her arms round me … I knew … I knew, she guessed, and then, I told her everything … she is good, so good, and Doag, loves you too and will do everything for us; I think my heart had broken long ago, if her dear tears had not been spilt to stay mine own."

Doag's face did not look very radiant, but "he supposed women must have confidants."

"Well," he continued, "meet me on the shore at three o'clock, and bring Mévanoui; perhaps your absence will be less remarked if you come not alone, and we will search for Father Jevan within his cell at Gwifen's shrine."

As immovable as the grey rocks that rose around him from the silted sand, a man stood waiting in St. Gwifen's bay. Half an hour, an hour, he stood thus attendant—the tide was rising rapidly, the little church, that had stood upon what was at first a promontory, was now quickly becoming insulated, as wave after wave ran in uproariously between the weed-covered rocks, till at last the causeway was completely submerged. The man was growing impatient: he strode across the sand to where sheltered in a dip of the greensward lay a boat. He pulled it down to the beach, unshipped the oars, looked at the weather … then a smile crossed his face, for he perceived two women coming down the hill, passing between the mounds of yellow gorse, walking rapidly towards him. They reached the boat—but now a strong southwesterly gale was dashing the spray over the boulders at their feet … Mévanoui turned white as she gazed seawards.

"Would you rather wait us here?" queried the bride. She did not answer with her lips, but a look of such unbounded relief relaxed her features, that the girl kissed her and stepped alone into the plunging barque, where her lover was waiting.

It was not more than a ten minute's pull, but such was the strength of the incoming tide, that they were tossed hither and thither, for what seemed, to the woman waiting on the shore, an hour of agony at least, but at last they reached the shingly beach of the little island, where a few yards from the water, perched upon a carpet of springy turf, stood the little chapel of Llan Gwifen,[22] served by

---

22. Llan Gwifen, a Christian hermit, of the sixth century, who raised, in this remote spot his little wattle chapelry, which was replaced in the twelfth century by a two-span church of some pretension.

Father Jevan, an old Welsh priest, one of that breed who long fought against the power of Norman Papacy.

Mévanoui saw them reach the door, and disappear within, and now she wished that she was with them.

All was dim inside, faint light came through the small windows, only the brass lamp swinging before the image of the Saint cast its yellow glow upon the incense-laden air. Near the stone altar Father Jevan knelt, but neither saw nor heard, as wrapped in spiritual ecstasy, he wandered in some golden maze of Paradise. The body, garbed in its brown habit, they grey head, the long grey beard, the moving lips, the inspired eyes were there—but the soul of Jevan walked beside his Lord in company with white-robed saints, through fields elisian; he heard the harps, the songs of praise, the murmur of the living streams of Heaven! … then … with a sigh, he tumbled back to earth … starting! … as he perceived his visitors … held up a hand in blessing … and advanced to meet the twain.

He had known Annesta since her babyhood, and loved her much, and questioned of her weary looks.

Then, in the silence of the dim-lit edifice, with halting sentences, the man and maid confessed their heinous sins.

Very stern, was the good Father … but slowly relented … Doag must profess Christianity, and be received within the bosom of the Church, Annesta make great expiation, weeks and months of penance only, could efface such a grave misdemeanour.

"But, ah, my children! human flesh is weak, and the serpent, our enemy, whispers echoes of Heaven into our ears that he may lure us thereby to hell! Watch and pray, pray and watch that ye fall not again at his bidding. O woman," he continued, turning to Annesta, "frail half of a great God's creation, sensuous and subtle, ever beckoning man to destruction, pray to the Mother of Christ to scourge the old Eve from your being."

Then he left them, that they might with tears and prayers plead for Heaven's forgiveness, promising to return in an hour, and join with the seal of the Church their illicit union.

As the evening sun poured in at the western windows, the words of the Latin service rolled over the kneeling couple. Annesta looked happier than she had done for months, but Doag's eyes were following the flight of the sea-gulls without, as they passed and repassed, now hurled by the wind 'gainst their wish, now beating laboriously up to it; to him their screaming seemed the solo to the anthem of an approaching storm, and the thin voice of the Priest as the strings of the harpist; he wondered how a man full of life and vigour could kneel within four stifling walls, pouring an endless stream of prayers before a stone altar, when the living God, the God of the universe, rode without on the wings of the wind, or rested, within the balm of the sun-laden air, where the honey-bee sucked in the clover! Why shut himself in this living tomb, whilst the wild sea broke on the boulders around him!

Now it was over; the good Priest was smiling upon them.

"May your union be blessed as that of Christ and his Church; may your children be many around you, and when the winter of life falls upon you, may they cherish and comfort your days, till you pass to God's keeping."

Madog bent his head; he felt the better for the blessing, the eyes that looked in his were pure and sinless, the face from out which they shone had been washed long ago from earthly dross … by tears innumerable…

Thus they were married—Madog and Annesta—Holy Church blessed their union, but non save the old Priest knew of their secret.

♪ ♪ ♪

Queen Crisiant had long cast lovelorn eyes at the young minstrel … nearly thrice his age though she was … a florid beauty yet clung to her and she hankered for the admiration she had received in her youth…. And this singer, with his great eyes, and voice of passion, stirred her inmost being, vibrating anew the slackening strings of her once lusting heart; but love turned to hate, as the eyes she would focus, wandered past hers, searching for those of one of her hand-maidens…. One day she called him to her.

"Doag," she queried, "to whom do you sing?"

"To all the Court, my lady; a minstrel has no early love. Music alone should be his mistress … for her he lives, to her he breathes his soul, whispering his passion, whimpering his pain. O Muse of beauty! O throb of all the spheres! O greatest gift of Heaven! the fairest legacy of man, his one remembrance of some former life of bliss, which vibrates through the world renewing hope of future happiness! … Philandre, to make the craven strong, physic unto the dying man … echoes which cheer our hearts, yet bring uncalled for tears! O love draught, making our pulse beat wonderingly.…" Suddenly ceasing his mad oraison he pulled himself together, his eyes yet shining with a light of half divine comprehension, he hesitate—ashamed of the feeling he had bared before the Queen.

Crisiant looked at him curiously.

"O Doag, Doag," she said, "is it not to you a very human muse? a muse all clothed in creamy flesh … with violet eyes?" She laid her hand upon his arm.… "A very human muse, whose self-same violet eyes have plombed your own and found her form reflected there? Say, Doag dear, are stolen kisses very sweet?" She stroked his cheek. Receiving no answer … "All women's kisses, 'sooth are much the same? if taken in the dark, I'll wager then, that you could never tell whose mouth it was that dragged the honey out of yours?" She was pressing close to him— Madog recoiled involuntarily, Crisiant bit her lip.

"Ugh, fool! ugh, silly fool; so Brenda's arms were soften then than mine!"

"Madam!" Madog started back, as if an arrow had found him.

"Poor stupid dolt, did you so gorge yourself with folly to think that I forget? You stroke a beard, and wear a well-tanned mask, but eyes! O eyes! … they are sad tell-tale tits…. We little dreamed that Brenda's lover would come back … but … having come, I wondered if another Queen would satisfy his heart!" shrugging his shoulders, "but 'tis the *muse*, the *fleshy muse*, you seek," scornfully. "No doubt our lord the King will welcome you, when he shall know that Brenda's paramour has now returned to snatch another she-lamb from his flock!" She paused … and laughed … and then went on again, "I give you just one month to change your mind," here she smiled warmly at him, "and if your mind be changed, and you will make for me a song more fair than ever you have made … for me alone—and sing it with your eyes feasting on mine, I will forgive your negligence, dear youth…. If not, ha! ha! his Majesty need not remain in ignorance that a young wolf feeds within his precious fold! and then he acts … as he thinks best! I bid you now Good-night." And with a mocking curtsey, Crisiant, Queen of Owain, swept away.

And Madog knew that Crisiant was given to no idle threats … that now the King was weak and ill, her will was his; and surely, too, the sick man had not long to live—he must speak soon, or never, and now the time seemed ripe to tell his parentage, be known as a Welsh Prince, ask ships for his great enterprise, and then, too, for his Annesta's sake, his birthright must be claimed … But how! who would believe … when Crisiant stood denouncing him, as Brenda's paramour!

He must see Pendaran, his old pedagogue and ask his help.

Obtaining leave of absence, Madog took horse next day, and rode toward the northern portion of the isle … rode till he saw Trysylwin mountain rise towering 'gainst the sky, and climbing up its rocky side reached Pendaran's cave in the early afternoon.

'Twas middle May and passing cold. He found the old Bard sitting by fire of wood. He rose, delight depicted on his face, to welcome his dear Madog once again; it was their first meeting for many years, for he had not been able to ride to see him since his return to Aberffraw.

There was so much to talk about, and when Pendaran heard his purpose, that he would disclose his name and ask for ships, his dim eyes filled with tears of joy.

"At last! at last! O Madog, I have waited long, yes all my life, and half of yours … and now … at last," lovingly he lingered on the words, "Now I may lay me down to rest … the purpose of my being all fulfilled … *I* may not see you more, your ships shall vanish one by one, beneath the vista of my world … You will have gone … but … of a surety I shall know the secret of the past is brought to man again."

Long the old Bard mused thus, seemingly content.

"Yes, yes, dear lad, I will commence at dawn my journey—and as fast as my gnarled limbs will carry me, speed south to Carno and see your mother's sire—for 'tis to him we look, he will announce your birth, and tell the story of your babyhood. Owain shall know the truth … O Madog, Madog … to-day you bring my pass to Liberty … I have held on tenaciously to life…. O heavy load, giving but wearing but weariness! … waiting, with lingering hope the hour of my release … Now, I may fold my wings and sink to rest."

♪ ♪ ♪

For hours they sat and talked and made all preparation for Pendaran to start early next day for Carno, to induce, if possible, Howel ap Jenaf to come north to visit Owain, and tell the truth about the Prince's birth.

chapter ix

the passing of owain

O N the southern rampart, wrapped in manny cloaks and skins, surrounded by his sons, his chiefs, his courtiers and his minstrels, lay King Owain dying. He had been brought up here to breathe the first warm air of summer (it was June). The dusk was falling.

Far away in the distance could be seen the sails of a small fleet beating up the bay, bearing the standard of Howel ap Jenaf, Lord of Arystli—at least so declared Llwyd the watchman.

"Why cometh he here?" whispered the sick man peevishly to Crisiant, "to reproach me on my death-bed for Brenda's sorrows," ... he paused ... "Brenda," he muttered again, as if the name cast some shadow of peace upon him. "Brenda ... perhaps soon I shall see you again ... hold you as first I held you ... in my arms".... he was silent ... a smile flickered over his grey features.

Crisiant, standing by the couch heard the hated name, and the dark blood spread across her face and neck. But she leant affectionately towards him and stroked his hand with her supple fingers.

"Dear lords," she whispered soothingly, "I am here," and bent to kiss his forehead; but a shudder ran through the frame of the old man, and he turned away.

She recoiled, but forcing a smile, beckoned to Madog to begin a song, lifting meanwhile a cup of cordial to Owain's lips.

"Drink, my lord, and listen on this new chaunt that Doag has for you?"

The King drank languidly and then sank back, plucking at the coverlet to pull it up yet higher over himself.

And Madog—as he watched the fleet glide ever nearer across the darkening sea—began his song, and he sang with such sweet melody, that for a moment Owain of Gwynedd sat upright again, clasping the ivory griffins of his couch … then … falling back with a sigh … closed his eyes, whilst across his face crept a light of ineffable peace; 'twas an old song, one that Brenda used to sing, when first he wooed her, in her father's home, far away … far away, 'cross Taranon mountain.

It was a love song, a pure love song, and had meant so much to him in those past days … days when he had so desired her, in the hours of his throbbing manhood … ah, those old times … when he and she had ridden together hawking over the Arystli hills, but even as he pondered, a mist of blood seemed rising before his eyes … for 'twas those same hills he had so lately sprinkled with her people's gore … when he had endeavoured to wrest Howel's patrimony from him. O God! how his life had been filled with warfare … warfare … warfare! how little truly love had ever brightened it … only of wantonness, repletion! … How many souls he had hastened to the brink … where to-night he stood himself … it seemed as if the armies of his dead were tramping across his burning brain with heavy rhythmical swing, drowning the minstrel's voice. Tramp, tramp, tramp! would they never cease! He lifted his hand wearily to his brow.

"O Wales! O Wales!" he murmured, "I have loved you so, and yet when I am gone, my sons will rend and slay tearing each other with bloody fangs, like soulless wolves, whilst grasping Normans plot to make them slaves … Will the Sun of Peace never dawn for Gwallia!" and even as he groaned, an echo of the minstrel's song pierced his fast clouding brain.

No blood shall dye the heather, no cruelty shall remain,
When we are wed together, blest peace alone shall reign.

"Poor maid … poor little maid" … whispered the dry lips, "she had hope … such hope … such foolish hope, that one could govern without war! in *Wales*!"…

For long he remained silent … endeavouring to follow the singer, but nearer than his voice another seemed hissing in his ear—

"King of Gwynedd! you have been a ware-wolf all your life…. mating with wolves … wolves alone have you begotten to reign after you!"

For a long time the old man lay quiet … struggling with death … trying to regain lucid thought.

"Brenda!" at last, he whispered. "Yes, you alone … you alone … yet there was none of our union … none … who born without fangs, in your image … might perchance have been upright, and ungrasping … as you were…" Then after a pause, "except a *cripple*," he muttered contemptuously, "a cripple! Princes can not be impotents!"

The singing had ceased, dusk lay upon the sea, as upon the land! Slowly emerging between two peaks of the great Snowdon range, rose up the summer moon, preternaturally large to-night it seemed, like some huge rayless sun. Up, up, it sailed, a golden ball lost in the purple sea of sky … below, upon the sand-dunes spread the mist … The sunset colours had all faded now, only upon the bryn the gorse still held reflexion of their staining!

The yellow moon, as it glided above the vapours of the earth—purged of her dross—was bleached to silver hue … and in her glory took possession of the world, insistent that her light alone should fill the eyes of man. Till reaching so great height, she spread her glittering mantle 'cross the bay, sending each wave a-rolling on the sands an argent bordured hem.

The fleet was nearing quickly now, ship after ship had crossed her silver track, until they reached the harbour of the Ffraw, and were half hidden at their anchorage below. On the ramparts all was silent, except for the heavy breathing of the dying King, and the occasional clank of harnessed men.

Madog sat at a distance, looking down towards the ships, where innumerable lights were beginning to twinkle … he was wondering if even now the message would be delivered before the end.

🎜 🎜 🎜

A distant blare of trumpets broke the stillness of the night. The clang of handled arms, hoarse shoutings of command, the tramping of mailed feet.

Soon a messenger was announced, who standing before Owain, spoke thus, that "Howel ap Jenaf, Lord of Arystli, over-lord of Ceirinion, vassal of the King, had come and would parley with the Prince; he came in peace, and would do obeisance, inquiring of his health."

"Tell him he may come," he whispered to Crisiant; "if he would curse me for the past it is of little moment now." He turned upon his pillows.

After the messenger was gone—within the hour—the braying of the horns grew louder, torch-bearers could be seen coming up the hill, then crossing the lowered draw-bridge, entering the Castle gate.

In the midst of his retainers walked the Lord of Arystli, with slow and faltering gait.

Upon the stone stairs the procession mounted. Then halting to reform, Howel could be seen, proceeding down the avenue of flaring light, towards the couch of his late enemy.

"Welcome, brother," whispered Owain; "we have fought, but now are friends … I have wronged you in the daughter you have to me, to love … cruel in the scorn of her childlessness … but Howel … you too know," he paused, straining for breath, "that 'tis the sacred duty of Kings to beget posterity!"

Tears were gathering in the eyes of the proud old man seated before Owain … his voice quivered so that he failed to frame the words he wanted to utter … and Crisiant, seeing the pause, to relieve the tension, beckoned to Madog.

"Doag, give a song to Howel, your old master, who sent you to Aberffraw!"

The young man rose, fingering his harp strings. The moon was now flooding sea and land with its splendour, illuminating the faces of the listeners, Doag alone stood in the shadow. Then he commenced … his head uplifted … his eyes, looking as it were, beyond the world, slowly the passionate notes rang out, treading the stillness.

My heard is hid in thee, my soul round thee entwined,
Thy whisper through the leaves, they dear breath in the air,
This earth, is heaven trod with thee, each moment fair.

Verse followed verse … till the last echoes died away … then Howel held up his hand.

"Owain, Owain," said he rising, and passing to the couch where the sick man lay, "Do you know who first sang that song?"

Was it a mist of tears, or the rime of death that was creeping before the King's eyes, that he could no longer see the figures around him?

"Brenda," he muttered hoarsely, "Benda, the maid you have me … she sang it … on her wedding night … long ago."

"Do you know, Owain Gwynedd, whom this singer is, who stands before you?"

There was silence … Howel was fighting against the bitterness of his soul … then with a mighty effort … gathering his forces, he cried out in a hoarse voice—

"This singer is the child you have to Brenda, this is Madog … your son, born in wedlock … *this* is the babe you would have murdered … had not Hunydd stolen him away, and carried him to Carno … *this* is the youth you would have slain in your wife's arms." … Then rapidly … whilst there was yet time, Howel unfolded the tale.

Crisiant, witting by with livid face, hardly able to control her feelings; Davydd, her son, who had come to his father's death-bed, standing behind his mother, with hate-distorted features, as revelation followed revelation, cursed all the saints beneath his breath.

Then Howel, having finished, laid his hand upon the King's.

"Owain," he said, "look at your son, do you acknowledge him?"

"I cannot see … the world's light has gone out for me … for ever … but this is truth you speak Howel ap Jenaf … he is my son, my lawful son by Brenda, this singer is Madog, a Prince of the House of Gwynedd … and God curse him … who shall deny all this. Impotent … unfit for reigning Prince … yet son of Owain, King of Gwallia. And I still give him, as his patrimony … the land this … side … of Snowdon…"

The effort was too much, Owain fell back, a stream of blood breaking from his lips, his attendants rushed to stay it, and lifting the frail form carried him down to his bed-chamber.

For some days the King still lived, but blind and deaf to the world … then … passed to his fathers…

A hundred messengers rod forth to spread the news through Wales.

🎵 🎵 🎵

A few months later, his solemn obsequies took place within the Cathedral church of Bangor; for now Becket had relented, the dead monarch was accorded Christian burial.

Thus by the high altar, they laid the warrior King—to sleep his sleep—in the presence of his thirteen sons, and a mighty host of Welshmen, and Howel ap Owain was proclaimed his father's heir, for Iowerth,[23] the elder, bore a scar across his face. But ere the ceremony ended one passed out with scowling countenance, vowing by "Cross of God," never to enter again those sacred portals except with the talaeth[24] of Gwynedd on his brow, and Crisiant blessed her son.

🎵 🎵 🎵

Howel, like Madog, had been fostered in the household of a Bard, one Kedivor. He was as brave and competent a soldier as his father Owain had been, but also a man

---

23. Any blemish precluded man from the Welsh succession.

24. Talaeth: the gold band or circle worn by the Welsh princes.

of learning, and much given to verse and song. The bond of music (at times stronger than the tie of blood) formed a link of friendship between him and his new-found brother Madog, whom he begged to return with him to Aberffraw and make it his future home—which Madog did—seeing what benefit it would bring to his wife, who had been delivered (in a neighbouring convent) of a child, a daughter, now three months old, whom she had christened Gwenllian.

For a whole year peace reigned in Wales.

Then came the news that Davydd had raised an army, and was threatening the kingdom, and that other princes had joined him.

So Howel and Madog, collecting their men, went out to fight.

A desperate battle ensued, ending in defeat for the two brothers.

Howel was killed by treachery, after the affray; Madog, who was wounded, escaped with a handful of followers to Aberffraw, which he quickly put in a state of defence, in preparation to withstand the siege he knew must follow; here he was joined by another brother Maelgwyn.

Meanwhile, Davydd the conqueror assumed royal power over all Gwynedd except in Môn.

By blood he had won his crown, by blood he meant to keep it; some of his brothers he murdered, others he imprisoned, only Madog and Maelgwyn remained untrappable in their island home.

To Aberffraw often came Pendaran, even urging Madog to leave the pack of Welsh wolf-princes to maul each other; entreating him, now he had little left to lose, to build a fleet and sail for the land of Druid legend, for said he—

"The legend is no legend, but the memory of our ancestors—grown dim perhaps with years—but true—our priesthood never lied … whence came the bands upon your arms? did not Heaven send the message across the waters calling you? Go now, whilst in the pride of manhood—whilst there is *time*," he whispered; "'tis a fair land, a peaceful land, Annesta and Gwenllian will be happy there, and you shall be king, a god perhaps, worshipped amidst a simple folk."

But Annesta did not wish to go; she grew cold at the thought of the wild elements, the ever heaving ocean, the endless track across the waters … and Madog dallied …

He begged patience of Pendaran; he was building ships for an expedition to Ireland, where he meant to claim for his brother Howel's sons the portion left them by their grandmother Pryvog.[25] When he should have accomplished this ... ah then ... he promised the old man, he would revictual those same ships, and start on *the great journey*.

Within six months his fleet was completed, armed, manned and victualled.

In the dusk of a summer night he sailed away towards the Irish coast, leading five of the vessels, in the *Annesta* (as he had named her), whilst Cadwallon, his chief captain followed in the *Gwenllian*, with the other five.

Ere distance grew too great, he turned for one last look towards his home. Yes, still she was standing there, that slim, fair figure of a woman, with an uplifted child, held arm high above her head ... the afterglow was lighting up the battlements, wet with recent rain, glazing them to crystal brightness, staining the sea beneath with roseate hues.

Thus in his memory enshrined, he ever after saw her.

---

25. Pryvog was an Irish princess.

Black clouds were hurrying up from the east, throwing the foreground into still higher relief, then came a scud of rain … blotting out Aberffraw … and it seemed, as though a veil of tears had descended to hide her from him.

Madog turned towards the vast waste of waters lying before, and drank a breath of salt sprayed wind, laughing with a new joy, as the good ship plunged and rose beneath him, shaking the foam from her bows like a rearing charger. A splash of green water broke awash and kissed his cheek … involuntarily his unfettered soul rose in a song of freedom, a song to the ocean his old love which the listening sea-gulls heard, and skrieched the chorus.

Night hid the tossing ships and darkening water from the woman on the battlements … she turned, clasping the child more tightly to her breast … descending the steps to the courtyard below … yet a great loneliness seemed falling on her … falling with the blackening night … was it darkness or tears what made her stumble?

chapter x

the cunning of wolf davydd

IT was a blustering day in March, some eight months later, that two musicians prayed admittance at the gate of Aberffraw. They were itinerants, travelling towards Ireland, singing their bread, as they journeyed thence. Times had been dull of late within the Castle, for the defenders, fearing treachery, had had little truck with the outer world.

After some parley, they were admitted, and proved no mean masters of penellion ... quick at the repartee, more than equal to the wit of Pecké, whose jokes through enjailment savoured of over-wear.

At supper time that time, the jest rang loud and merry, wine loosened tongues; even Maelgwyn's sad countenance was cleared and Annesta smiled, as she wrote words of love to Madog, words the singers swore to take her lord, when they should cross the sea next day, and bear faithfully to the encampment where he bode, awaiting spring to end his enterprise.

And as the evening hours wore on, most fell asleep where they had supped, or went to rest. The two musicians reeling towards the common chamber of the guests, lurched up against the guard-house door, where they paused, and hammering, called for a last drink of mead.

"No, not unless you tell us some fresh tales!" Which promising to do, they gained admittance, and yarned, and yarned away, until the merry guards were nigh to bursting with their piquant jokes!

But as one spoke, the other, seeming drunk, dropped quietly into foaming tankards a few gouttes of atropa ... quickly the poison worked ... until around them lay a crew of senseless men.

Then ere the pigeons rose to call from roost, two figures crept towards the gates, raised the portcullis, and let down the bridge ... quickly across its girders hissed the *frousse* of eager feet, and part of Davydd's army crawled within the camp.

Then was a hue and cry, the shouts of garrison surprised! The yells of wounded men, the shrieks of fearsome womenfolk!

The flagstones of the court were weltering in blood.

Maelgwyn, who had rushed out at the first sound of tumult, was cornered, and fighting like a madman, fell pierced at last, like to some furious hedgehog, bristling with spears. Fiercely they fought, scarce knowing friend from foe.

Then as the dawning broke, the hubbub slowly ceased, and Davydd, wiping his red sword, bade all his captains to the banquet hall, where still the remnants of the last evening's supper lay.

Having secured by strategy the last stronghold of his enemy and being thus undisputed King of Gwynedd, he took up his residence at Aberffraw.

And here, it was his evil intent to undertake a different sort of conquest ... one, not of the sword, but of the heart!

Long years ago, ere the coming of Madog, Davydd had loved Annesta, the Queen his mother's lady; he had loved her secretly, casting his covetous gaze upon her comely form; his lustful eyes had fed upon her flesh (sending cold shivers thro' *her* soul), his breath had scorched her cheek, his sensuous touch filled her with loathing ill-concealed! ... but now ... *his* turn had come. The scorning woman was his prisoner, lying within his power, to crush ... to soil ... to work his will upon ... he licked his water lips ... and spat upon his palm, and rubbed it gleefully. "And Madog," he chuckled, "what just repayment of old scores!"

That night Davydd sent for his captive, requesting her to sup with him.

And she, knowing the fruitlessness of refusal, accepted his invitation, went in and sat beside her conqueror, who plying her with viands, talked to her of poetry, song, and other arts he knew she loved; drank ever to her eyes, displaying such respect she was amazed at his new gentleness.

And so the days went on. Davydd ever in attendance doing his utmost to please his caged bird … and though at heart she hated him, she tried to think she judged him harshly.

He sent for his musicians (some of the most skilled in Wales!), he gave her costly robes and jewels—which she, constrained to take, quickly resigned to waiting maids!

He played with Baby Gwenllian as *if* he loved her.

But notwithstanding this and much other courtly attention, he kept her prisoner; no news of Madog pierced her solitude to bring her hope.

Plans of escape she daily schemed, doomed to miscarriage all.

Then one night Davydd taxed her banteringly.

"Why do you wish to fly, dear lady? Am I not kind? I, your most natural protector when Madog is away? Why not treat me as a brother?" His lips were close to her, they touched her forehead … they burned themselves into her skin, it seemed as though a raven fouled her flesh … she started back … he caught her in her arms. "Annesta," he whispered fiercely in her face "you *know* I love you." His bloodshot eyes seemed searing out her soul … his features were convulsed with passion! Then as suddenly as he had seized her, he let her go—and turned away.

Sick and faint, she sank back in her chair; he had hidden his face in his hands, but she could see the veins, like whipcord, standing out in his coarse neck.

For several days afterwards she feigned illness, and kept to her apartments.

Then one morning, when the sun shone with unwonted brightness, and the wind blew from the south, she walked upon the battlements to take the air, in company with her companions … but alas, only to come face to face with her tormentor. He, very pale, saluted her.

"Madam, the day was bright before, but not so bright as since you came! I pray you spare me some of your sweet leisure, and send away your ladies, that I may the more enjoy it undisturbed." A courteous demand … yet bearing no refusal, for two of his captains escorted her women down the steps, leaving the two alone. Then sitting on the parapet, he drew her to him with iron strong wrists, placing his face near hers.

"How long, Annesta, do you intent to treat me thus? Will you defy for ever, denying all I ask? Must I use force? or will you graciously consent to be my … my love? Oh the old days were nought to this," he hissed passionately, holding her tightly. "You are more beautiful in motherhood, than ever as a girl. O God! I love you so … and you …

you *shall* be mine, living or dead." She could not restrain a groan, he was holding her so fast. "Dear love," he pleaded bending down, "be kind." He paused, then tentatively in her ear, "if not, I also can be cruel;" his eyes glinted with malice. "Do you love Gwenllian? What if she died! Oh, children often die, young children—a curdled milk! A careless nurse! You shudder, but accidents oft befall the banes of kings." He watched her from the corners of his eyes; "but give your love, and not a hair of Gwenllian's head, but shall grow as long as yours,—enough to-day ... perhaps I am too premature ... too pressing in my pleading for your heart ... goodbye ... goodbye ... my soul's desire." He stopped exultingly, but ... as if the impulse were too strong to withstand, he bent down, taking her face between his hands, kissed her upon the mouth, the eyes, the forehead—then turned and left her ... to summon her companions once again.

Two nights later, Baby Gwenllian was let down from a turret window, to an emissary of Pendaran's, to be quietly spirited away to the cave on Trysylwin mountain.

Next day the met, and Davydd tried to steal a kiss, she smote him with her woman's might across his hated his mouth.

A few quiet days were hers ... and she! ... she began to hope her persecution ended! ... or if not ... well—he might kill her now that Gwenllian was safe ... and death, she brooded bitterly, were surely preferable to this daily contamination … "God grant dishonour come not first!" Ah, surely Madog must return soon! Full of new hope each dawn; … stayed by fresh faith each fall; the helpless woman prayed and waited.

♩ ♩ ♩

One night she lay and dreamed that she was free again, playing with Gwenllian near to Pendaran's cave. Below stretched out the rippling sea, around the sea-gulls hovered screaming;—turning over, till their white wings—touched by the sun-rays—appeared like silver. How they two romped together, the pungent odour of wild thyme, crushed by their feet, mounting upon the morning air.

How joyously they tumbled on the turf, the short sweet turf! Baby Gwellian's rippling shouts rivalling the gull's! How good it was to be free once more! … free from the jail-like Castle.. and the haunting face of the lusting one! Ah, how soft was the little hand that tugged at her hair! that caught at her breast! Annesta smiled as she dreamed!

♩ ♩ ♩

A figure of a man, wrapped in a long cloak, was crossing the courtyard, in the gloomy stillness, walking rapidly towards the guarded portico of the corridor which led to the women's apartments—where slept the Lady Annesta.

Sharply the challenge rang out.

"Who goes there?"

"The King." Then all was quiet again.

Stealthily the footsteps continued down the passage, at the end of which was a nail-studded door ... the man lifted the latch, and peered within ... it was in darkness, save for the light of a silver lamp which swung before a crucifix, the draught from the door made it flicker.

On a canopied bed in the centre, beneath an embroidered coverlet, lay a woman, the light illuminating her face. She appeared to be dreaming ... she smiled ... she moved ... raised her arms, from which the white shift fell, revealing the strong fair flesh ... she smiled again ... and whispered, "Gwenny," then turned over to the darkness.

The other figure stood silently watching, his face, the face of a lusting ram ... he clenched and unclenched his hands.... his eyes were burning in his head ... great beads of sweat were breaking on his forehead; he moved closer to the sleeping woman ... put out a hand ... touched the bosom that was bare.

"Baby," she smiled again, "Baby" ... He knelt beside the couch ... her breath was fanning his cheek ... he placed his arm beneath the supple form ... Annesta's eyes opened, shining with a light of happy wistfulness ... then ... and as the brain began to work, and she slowly comprehended—they filled with unutterable horror … She sprang up with a terrified shriek … He caught her and pressed her down.

"Annesta," he muttered, "I *love* you." He was holding her like a vice … in his embrace, his warm body next to hers … She struggled like one demented in her mad terror … but what was her strength to his!

Crunch … he had broken her arm … but what matter! insane in his furious passion … he knows … he feels, nothing but his unholy desire…. Snatching a pillow he presses it over her face, to quell her crying … a sudden quiver … a sensation … then she falls limply back amidst the coverings … he has conquered … Panting! throbbing in every pulse … the thick veins of his forehead projecting like ropes … his muscles trembling from the fight … Davydd stands beside his prey.

Why does she continue to lie so still? has she swooned? He bends and listens for her breathing … certainly it is faint, he cannot hear it … drowned by the beatings of his own heart, no doubt!

He lifts her arms … it falls down again … he puts his hand upon her breast … but there is no fluttering movement discernible … A great horror seizes him…

"Good God, she can't be dead!" He touchers her hand again, it is nerveless and strangely limp. A sudden panic grips him … this blood-stained soldier of many wars …

a fear of the quiet form lying before him! A woman ... a woman he loves ... not done to death! ... he had never slain a woman yet! ... Then hurriedly he covered her up, as he had found her an hour ago ... and stealthily passed from the chamber, closing the door ... nothing appeared disarranged ... he walked rapidly along the corridor ... and out into the night ... he passed the guards unchallenged ... how quickly the clouds were scurrying over the face of the moon!

Throwing off his cloak, without undressing, he lay down upon his couch ... but he could not sleep ... sometimes he was shivering, sometimes burning. It was stifling within walls ... he rose and went upon the battlements, but the night wind came howling up from the sea, and chilled him to the marrow ... he went down again and sought the deserted banqueting hall ... he must have wine.. he drained a tankard of strong mead, then another ... yet another ... ah, that was better ... it soothed his senses, and quieted them ... then he groped his way somewhat unsteadily back to his room ... and lay upon his bed again. A short heavy sleep ... then waking with a start ... returning reason shows him dawning day ... the sparrows are twittering ... a pigeon pluming its feathers upon his window ledge ... how he hates pigeons...

Now the Castle life is waking, he hears the shuffling of many feet ... there seems to be much whispering ... now—O God ... there are cries ... then shoutings...

Will no one ever come his way? Yes, some one has entered; he covers his head…

"Sire, Sire," cries Anarawd, his favourite captain, "the Lady Annesta is dead!"

chapter XI

madog's home-coming

OR three days a furious storm had been raging in Cardigan Bay. On the morning of the fourth a small fleet might be seen beating its way laboriously up from the west, apparently running for shelter towards the mouth of the Dovey.

At last … one by one, the tempest-tossed vessels weathered the point, and passed into the quieter waters of the land-locked estuary; swiftly they came, borne on the incoming tide, which swirled and eddied as it met the out-flowing river.

Around—mottled alternately with cloud and sunshine—lay the green hills.

It was a beautiful morning, fresh and wild, the softness of spring yet held in check by the boisterous breath of winter.

Madog had intended to sail straight from Ireland to Aberffraw, but the weather had been too much for him, and he had had perforce to run in here, to wait for calmer seas.

As the ships came sailing in, a traveller could be seen, attended by two men in harness, riding along the coast, bearing in his arms a child; and, as he rode, he watched them wonderingly.

"Say, Humphrey," he queried, is it not the banner of Madog that they bear, surely 'tis his griffin bellying in the wind?"

"Aye, aye, my lord, so it appears to be."

The old man lowered his hand, it strained his eyes watching the ships amidst the dancing sunlight of the waters.

"Strange fate," he mused, "that should bring the returning expedition as to a trysting place!"

Pendaran—for it was he—was flying with Gwenllian to Carno to escape her mother's murderer, and his way took him from Aberdovey to Machynlleth along the coast.

Later in the morning, when the vessels lay tugging at their hawsers in the swiftling tide, and the worn-out mariners—changed of their sopping clouts—were making merry over their mid-day meal, Madog sat alone in the stern, droused by the sunshine, lulled by the swill of the passing of the passing waters—watching the sea-gulls idly, as they fought for scraps of meat. He was wondering how soon he should see Annesta again ... and afterwards ... how soon (according to his promise) he should, re-caulked and re-victualled, set sail on that adventurous voyage to the unknown land of Druid legend ... bearing with him wife and child.

"And yet," he sighed, as his eyes travelled along the undulating line of the coast, "O thou beautiful land of Wales, thou home of my race, land of wild mountains, land of boisterous streams—I love thee with my heart's blood ... but I must see thy heather red with gore, thine eagles flying from the shrieks of brawling men, thy reigning princes, surly dogs, born out to yap and snarl!" His gaze wandered across the strip of blue water to the surrounding hills, golden with furze embroidered in their green ... shining with hawthorn, white amidst the trees ... he saw the wet sand spreading out beneath, waiting the kiss of coming waves.

"O Gwallia, Gwallia! land of disorder! land of the war shout! will peace *ever* come to thee—at last?" Strong man that he was, he bit his lip to keep down the tears that were near rising.

As thus he moralized, he became aware that a coracle had put off from the shore, and seemed to be making for the ships; now and anon the eddies caught it, and whirled it round, but soon it was righted and started on its way again, ever approaching nearer.

An old man was the only occupant, paddling with practised skill.... As he came within the hail, Madog recognized Pendaran, who a few minutes later, had reached the side of the barque, and was being hauled up by the horny-fisted seamen.

"Pendaran, old friend," said Madog advancing to meet him, "you are indeed a welcome sight, for you can give me news of home. What luck has brought you south-ward? You could not know that I was coming here ... to bring me salutation!"

A dark flush spread across the old man's face. "O Prince, 'tis an ill welcome that I bring to-day; the dogs of hell are loose and wandering o'er the earth, their fangs dripping with blood ... your people's blood."

"What say you?" said Madog, springing up from the coil of rope on which he had seated himself again.

"O lord, my dear, dear lord ... your palace, even Aberffraw is but a charnel house, that stinks of dead ... reeking with the accursed."

"Annesta?" he hissed through his teeth, shaking the old man roughly by the shoulder, "where is she?"

"Sire," he paused ... his grey beard buried on his chest, his eyes abased, "she is not here, but gone to that blest land beyond the stars."

"Dead! not dead? ... O my beloved!" ... For a time the man stood, deaf and sightless, then suddenly, as if a new and horrible thought had crossed his brain, he clutched at Pendaran's arm ... "Dead ... *dead* ... not? ... thank God she's *dead* ... tell me," he whispered with dry gasps, "*how* ... Annesta ... died?"

Pendaran's face grew black again.

"My lord, they say" ... he hesitated ... "they say ... that when her ladies ... went to wake her ... they thought her sleeping ... but found that she was dead ... The King's herbalists sware 'twas an affection of the heart. Davydd makes great pomp, and will have her laid in the Cathedral Choir of Bangor, in front of high altar, where your father lies" ...

"*Davydd?* curst limb of hell, I would that I could grip you now, tear your vile tongue from out your lustful maw ... burst of those lewd eyes ... brand murderer on your cheek ... 'twas as *his* captive ... the fear of him ... that sapped my true love's life ... she knew that his desires burned towards her ... was afraid ... afraid of his vile love ... thank Heaven ... that she is *dead*!"

Lifting his hands to the skies Madog invoked every bitter curse upon his half-brother's head. Then, as one exhausted, sank down again upon the pile of cordage.

"Gwenllian," he whispered, "my little one!"

"My lord, she is even now in a hut on yonder shore; return with me, and take her in your arms ... poor babe ... sans mother."

"Maelgwyn?"

"Sire, he too was slain, pricked through with many spears, a wall of dead piled up around."

Thus Pendaran gave his message, but dared to breathe no word of whispers culled about Annesta's fate.

At even, he and Madog went ashore and baby arms were locked about the father's neck ... by unaccustomed softness bringing tears ... which having brought, she cried herself to sleep in childish sympathy.

That night,—Madog, Pendaran and Cadwallon—sat long discussing future plans ... whilst Gwenllian slept, upon a bed of bracken, near the fire.

Swayed by black hate and fury towards Davydd, Madog and Cadwallon matured ever schemes of bitterest revenge, bitter retribution, impracticable for weak men over strong ... as hours crept on, the Bard sat silently, tendering only halting advice, when asked—professing but respectful interest in all their arguments. Then—when all possible means of retaking the island and driving out the present occupiers of Aberffraw had been discussed and re-discussed, and the two men were almost growing angry with each other over heated parleying, even as the grey dawn brightened the lintels of the door, Pendaran arose and stood before the desperate plotters.

"Ten vessels and three hundred men! Madog of Gwynedd! has your most natural passion of revenge so blinded your campaigning eyes? Is Davydd some young chicken? or fox of cunning ... serpent of wisdom! when a great stake is at issue? And these brave men—O Madog! who've followed you through many an Irish fight, you'd lead them back to death—or torture—for some fiends squirm gleefully to see the quivering flesh torn from the captives' bones!" he whispered. "O Prince, son of my spirit, conception of my soul, drop this mad enterprise; Heaven's curse shall rest on Davydd—the gods are just—in poverty and exile shall he die—and King's son, bite the dust in ravening hunger. Do you remember, a great promise that you made to me? ... now ... now's the time. Oh, my dear lord, commander of a fleet ... the day for the great realization of your life has dawned! Your ships lie rocking in the estuary. Your crews are eager for adventure—revictual and set out ... 'tis spring, Heaven favours you, fair winds shall haste ... and then, beyond the sea, a new bright life awaits you, a life unstained with blood."

Thus, the old man pressed ever his advantage. Madog was obdurate at first, his fingers itching for the veins of Davydd's throat. He had come back from Ireland, seeking home and wife, and this damned thief, who'd stolen both was living yet!

"Nay, old Pendaran," he said, bringing his fist down on the bench, "a man can die but once, and if I have to go alone to Aberffraw, and enter in disguise to murder him, my last breath shall be sweet … but … leave it all, and think he breathes, that hound of hell…" he spat upon the ground.

"So you will go and kill yourself in Môn, and leave your corpse one evening's tasty supper for his dogs? … will your Annesta—dreaming in Hath-Innis[26]—be one white nearer to your heart that night?" He laid his hand upon the young man's sleeve. "Oh, let the soiled and gory past bury itself; leave no more carcases to foul this blood-stained land of ours; you shall pass westward cross the seas, and then be King over a land to which all gwallia is but a Cantref's breadth in size—a very Eden upon earth—the Hesperides of ancient lore; and some day, you shall homeward turn again, and gather sons of Wales to your new fold! The east has waited for six thousand years, remembering this country of the west—six thousand years have waited for to-day!—destiny hangs pregnant, craving your helping hand! There is nought now to keep you here; I will take Gwenllian to Howel at Carno; her pattering steps shall cheer his lagging ones. He will provide her marriage dower, and care for her in times to come. A bloody hand has streaked across the

---

26. Hath-Innis: the Paradise of Druidism

pages of your past, and left them beautiless, your friends are gone ... your island stronghold lost ... your wife ... your wife is *dead*..."

Three days he dallied!

Then parleyed with his crews, and found them willing (had not Pendaran bribed them with dream of gilded cities, vestures rich and gems ... graving each heart with tales of fairyland!). Yes, they would follow Madog to new life.

Thus setting to their work, they cleaned the bottoms of their ships, filling their holds with water, wine, dried meats ... dried fish, flour and much cheese, and all that hunger-dreading men might want!

After ten days of strenuous labour, the fleet of sail was ready, and as the sun rose on the middle day of May, Madog set his canvas and went forth; leading on half of the ships, whilst Cadwallon followed with the rest. Southward they bore, leaving the Welsh coast on their port, till at eventide they passed by Ynysyr-Hyrddod, and knew to a man that it was the last sight of Wales their eyes might ever catch.

The rays of the setting sun emblazoned to blood-red hue the surrounding waves, as rising and falling the well freighted ships passed over the swirling waters; and now, as they steered westward it seemed as though they passed down a road of scintillating light, a legacy of the sinking orb, who ere he disappeared, had laid a track to guide them to that mystic land towards which he ever homed.

Then Madog, standing in the prow of the *Annesta*, lifted his arms towards the glory, and prayed the great Life Spirit for guidance in his quest;—and as he prayed the sleeves of his tunic slipped back, displaying the golden bands that encircled them, until they too caught the radiance, and shone as circles of living fire.

"O Armlets of the Sun," cried the freed man, "I am taking you back to the land from whence you came." … Thus he stood in contemplation, till night was come; his crew watched him, fascinated by this lonely, fateful figure silhouetted against the waning light, approaching not, till the mantle of darkness had quite descended.

Now they knew that only the open sea lay beyond, realized that they were passing from the old world … perhaps for ever … passing … whither?

The mast-head lights were twinkling like fire-flies, the only gleams amidst profoundest gloom…!

Thus, went out from Europe a few picked men of Wales, into the unknown, with stars alone as guides;

chartless, except for Druid legend; but to Madog, the wind that sobbed in the rigging seemed the echo of Pendaran's chauntings, urging him on, blessing him, promising that 'twas no fool's errand on which he adventured … that 'twas not to fill the ever hungry maw of death that he had embarked these trusting men!

"'Pendaran,' he whispered, 'do you know?'"

chapter XII

beyond the confines of humanity

FOR weeks the days passed on monotonously. 'Twas now a month since they had sailed. Sailed, ever helped by steady winds from north-east, south-east or from east; winds favourable to Madog's enterprise, and wonderfully the vessels had kept near together too.

During the day, the Prince would sit in the watch tower high up the mast, straining his eyes for hoped-for land … but ever was the sun set, it disappeared behind an endless vista of heaving waves, and boundless, trackless waters … at dawn he would climb up again, with momentary hope, but 'twas only a bank of blue grey clouds that lay athwart the west not misty mountain tops.

Ever the ships were moving onward, yet, day in … day out … no change. Till it had seemed as tho' they passed beyond all space, into infinity, beyond the confines of the world, as if their toiling was but vain!

At last their hearts grew faint—slowly but surely they lost faith … and then began to grumble … first murmuring sullenly beneath their breath … whilst uneventful days passed vacuously … no change appeared … all their drear world a watery waste!…

Two months were gone … and then, they came to Madog saying—"They'd done enough—could no more … *would* do no more … 'twas only tempting Providence … they had reached a world beyond God's sphere … beyond which, existence doubtless was impossible … a world beyond the limits of humanity!"

Madog could give no answer. His sad eyes travelling west, then turning on his heel, he went below.

Cursing their leader, the discontented mariners signalled to the *Gwenllian*, and the other ships, telling their comrades—all was finished now, they *would* turn back … or mutiny. Which, Cadwallon learning, entered a boat and came off to the *Annesta*. There he found Madog desperate, brooding disconsolate within his cabin door.

He tried to comfort him, but knew, comfort he could not give.

Then leaving the man with his shattered hopes, the ever resourceful Cadwallon made his way to the surly crew.

"Men," he said, "you have come so far believing in the promise of the Bard Pendaran, Pendaran the unacknowledged Druid, descendant of those faithful priests who ever led your race in prosperous times (before the cursed hosts of Rome swarmed conquering through your land). They—these same Druids, held alone the knowledge of the past, the world before the flood, and 'tis the spirits of your forebears that cry to you today, enjoining you to seek afresh the land, which was the cradle of your race. Ye cannot see it yet but it is *there*," he pointed westwards. "Give him, this emissary of Pendaran, just one day more; if still the fates be opposite we will retrace our tracks to blood-stained Wales."

So with strong words Cadwallon dragged their unwilling promise from the crew.

"Madog," he said returning, and laying a hopeful hand upon his shoulder, "one day of grace I have extorted … after that!"

🎜 🎜 🎜

Next dawn, the sun rose on a rippleless sea, an endless mirror reflecting but a brazen sky. No breath of air to fill the flapping sails, or temper the hot morn.

"Heaven is against me," Madog sighed, as he stood gazing down into the unfathomable waters. Then as the burning day dragged on to evening time, he stood before his men, and gave commands—"At sunset—put about."

Then going to his cabin, flung himself face downwards on his couch a victim to despair.

But even as he lay, searching the dead future for some spark of hope, a bank of clouds was rising on the horizon, and then came scurrying up from out the east—and ere the sunset time had gone, it was as though volumes of black smoke had rolled up in the sky … a flash of lightning, followed by a thunderous roar—until it seemed, the heavens themselves must split and break!

The howling wind soon caught the staggering ships within his grasp, and lashing them with fury, turned them round and round, like autumn leaves in mountain spate! Now up to heaven he drew them, then hurled them down to hell again, till creaking from stem to stern, they groaned for mercy; the white sea-horses tearing at their sides, flinging themselves hungrily across their decks as if to catch the human units, that ran hither and thither, clinging to pars and masts, as they endeavoured to haul in the fast tattering sails.

At his cabin door stood the man who had risked all to bring his fellow-men to such a plight!

Fascinated—he watched them, in their impotent haste; he looked at the angry seas, the hell black skies … but the glint of sullen despair had gone.

"If this be death," he muttered, "welcome death! … but if … but if…" … he smiled, the shrieking wind drowned his words in its thunder … but he knew that the mad tempest that laughed at the men … was bearing them westwards.

Between the howling gusts, he could catch snatches of the crew praying to St. Cyric—"Blessed St. Cyric, hear and deliver us! O Saint of mariners hush the storm, smooth the sea! Preserve us thy humble worshippers from the perils of deep waters!" It was the cry of dying men, men without hope, tottering on the threshold of chaos, pausing to pray ere they plunged o'er the brink of the world, into eternity!

Five days they called upon his name, sport of the inferno of mad raging seas. Was the storm-god all too powerful? or were they derelicts already, beyond the confines of the Calendar—lost souls, whose cries might never pierce again those realms where rest the blessed saints!

"St. Cyric, oh, St. Cyric, forgive our sins, and bring us back to land; we do repent, and we will build a house unto thine honour—upon the shore—and offer masses to thy name—as long as we shall live, O great St. Cyric, Saint of the Sea!"

And thus they prayed, believing this battle of the elements a fierce warfare 'twixt the sea-gods and the saints … for their poor human souls! Five days of buffeting … and Cyric then prevailed … a patch of blue appeared through the black clouds.

Rocked in the cradle of a kinder sea, the battered mariners sat about the sopping decks … worn out … indifferent now to fate; exhausted by their struggle with the deep.

To-day their vessels rolled up an after swell, one hundred furlongs further off from Wales, and too far now, ever to return without revictualling!

Seven ships only clung together, where once there had been ten!—tattered and mastless ... like dark water birds ... striving to keep in touch.

And the sailors, cursing their folly for having believed Pendaran, and followed Madog, showed their discontent in their sullen faces.

Three days' victuals remained, the fresh water was already all consumed ... but yet ... there must be wine. Ah, happy thought ... and breaking in the holds they dragged the wine skins out from the great belly of the ship ... and drank ... and drank their fill!

Ah, life was good again—what mattered perils, with that new sense of sunshine creeping through their veins!

And so they soaked, and soaked, till sleep enwrapped them in most blissful dreams—or fought and fondled, singing ribald songs, chasing each other round the slippery decks!

♪ ♪ ♪

Madog, with aching heart, climbed the mast-head to his old eerie tower, and wrapping himself within his cloak, sat thinking through the night.

"So *this* was how death crept to him!—no border fight ... no murderer's knife ... simply to be rocked in the trough of summer sea—whilst hunger gripped his entrails ... and burning thirst parched his dry throat ... swayed idly at the ocean's will ... to and fro ... fro and to ... swung to eternity, upon the cradle of the gods!"

At last dawn broke ... he did not move ... "Dawn," he muttered contemptuously, as the light spread slowly across the sky—"Ah, in the days gone by, at the first changing of the black to grey, his eager eyes had strained towards the west! but now ... How welcome that one dawn should be that found those eyes fast glazed in death ... death ... that should of a surety bring him rest at last."

Fair Hope was dead, Despair reigned now as queen!

The sun was well above the horizon, when Madog, son of Owain, stretched his still limbs, and standing up with haggard face turned towards the east, thought of the endless seas dividing him from Wales.

He wondered if the mists lay thick in Carno vale. Whether the sun was visible above the Clorin yet, touching the towers of Howel ap Jenaf's holt ... flooding the woods with light....

Had the good Hospitallers passed to church—chanting their psalms? Then tears of weakness gathered in the eyes of the starving man.

"Ah, death," he prayed, "come soon, for so the sorrows fall in life, that thou becom'st the greatest benediction ever bequeathed by gods to men…. I have no further wish but to become, one with the sea and air, filter of sunshine, breath of stormy wind … I pray oblivion—blessed dissolution…."

Thus idly musing, Madog gazed upon the sea beneath.

Suddenly, something arrested his attention. What was that strange object he beheld borne on the breast of the waves? now rising … now sinking … reflecting the glint of the morning sun? Some hideous monster of the deep … nosing the carrion soon to be thrown to him! or a spectre of his disordered brain? Some hallucination born of hunger? He pressed his eyes, then looked again … Was it madness coming before death? Sometimes it appeared to be like a floating tree! with green leaves still attached … sometimes like mane of seaweed on a gorgon's pate…. His head was reeling … he *must* be going mad.

Rubbing his eyes he looked again…. Great Baal! … it *was* a tree! … or he were dreaming … he hit his breast to wake himself … he would go nearer….

Clinging tremblingly (for he was very weak) to the ratlines, he crept downwards to the deck … went to the taff-rail and looked over … the object was floating close by, as they passed it … it *was* … it *was*, a tree … root, leaves and all … as if torn up by some wild hurricane.

Excitement held him dumb: his mouth was dry and parched, his black tongue swollen. Holding on to death's skirts, hope came and pushed him away, and showed him *this*! this sign of life … he looked around … the sailors were lying about in semi-sodden torpor still; wretched they appeared after their night's debauch, dirty and sick, in the clear light of day.

He could not shout … his voice had long grown weak from deprivation … he could not raise it above a whisper … yet, his heart was bursting to bring this new-born hope to the wretched handful of despairing human beings … this promise of earth which must be near!

As he stood on the deck, faint, with the warm blood reflowing through his torpid veins, once more he leaned against the side, to look over, to be quite sure … Yes, a tree it was, and nothing but a tree … then, staggering towards the steersman, who stood doggedly by his helm—

"Llowerch," he whispered, "Llowerch, look!"

The man grinned imbecilely.

"Llowerch … it is here at last. Heaven has guided us…" Sullenly the man turned his bloodshot eyes in the direction to which the chief pointed … then … suddenly comprehending … he fell upon his knees, pouring volley after volley of blessing on the good St. Cyric ... and stumbling up, rushed like a maniac round the decks amongst his drowsy comrades, shaking and kicking them into being.

Like a hive of bees, disturbed, they swoon swarmed about the ship, climbing aloft ... looking over the side at the strange floating giant ... or scanning the long neglected horizon!

Quickly they signalled the news to the other ships. The log was taken in tow, whilst branches of its green leaves were lopped—and lashed to masts, and sterns, and bows, decking the derelicts like festal galleons!

What little canvas they had managed to repair after the gale, they spread, running before an ever-freshening breeze.

Such watching followed as never was before; in turn each sailor climbed the masts, and stayed his time; the next one greedy of his place, for had not Madog offered a hundred pieces of red gold to him who first should sight the longed-for land!

After three days of ceaseless straining towards an ever heaving horizon, even Welsh eyes grew tired. Madog, alone, never missed his vigil, and to him came the reward; for, as dawn broke upon the fourth, his eyes—almost blind with gazing—beheld a grey undulating line of hills, rising from the waste of waters. And he ... turning towards the newly risen sun, now rolling up in the eastern sky, lifted his bare arms ... encircled with the brine-dimmed bands of gold, which, sea-stained though they were, yet caught and reflected the brilliancy of the first solar rays.

"Pendaran," he whispered, "do you know?" And it seemed to him as if the words echoed around the world, as if an exultant shout of triumph was wafted back, reverberating the shoutings of a million waiting souls amidst the rushing of the spheres.

♪ ♪ ♪

Two days later, the *Annesta* and *Gwenllian*, with the rest of the fleet, lay at anchor in a sun-lit bay; around them—hither and thither—darted many strange canoes of bark, filled with swarming bronzed humanity … whose curiosity, overcoming fear, bartered fruits for coloured clothes, or water and milk for beads and trinkets.

♪ ♪ ♪

In a short space of time, when the starved sailors had somewhat recovered their strength, they launched their coracles, and explored the coast, finding the country both beautiful and fertile. Then after some weeks, the chief and some dozen followers were conducted by friendly natives on a fourteen days' march inland, to a city of pretension and magnificence—to which those they had known in

Wales were mean indeed; even Caerleon was small and poor in comparison.

Vast palaces and temples rose, with marble cupolas, flashing in the sun; pyramids—such as Madog had visited in Egypt, marked the tombs of their dead kings.

The streets were broad and clean—and the populace seemed orderly.

Madog, Cadwallon, and such of their companions who had accompanied them, were taken before the Emperor of the country, who received them with marked pleasure, treating them as heaven-sent beings, beings from another world.

(Ah! Pendaran's stories were but dreams to this reality! It was a new earth indeed to these half savage Welshmen, who had never tasted luxury—and the thoughts that turned to their distant fog-crowned mountains, and vales of bloody feud, were not wholly of regret!)

And so they settled in the country—some in the city, some near the coast,—and there—amidst a fringe of palm-trees on the shore, they raised the Chantry to St. Cyric's cult, that good blest saint, who'd wrested them from sea-god's wrath, and wafted them to such a pleasant land.

Cadwallon brought the natives Christ; and taught them all the name-days of the saints, and how to pray to God.

And as the years went on, many exiles married women of the land, and when the babes were born, baptized them with the sign of the holy cross. But Madog (ever son of nature in his heart) showed them the arts and crafts, that he had learnt from many countries, in his voyages in far seas; and told them of the wisdom of the Bards, inheritors of ancient Druid cult—also—he told them "The Old Tale," belief in which had brought him, and this handful of his followers, across the trackless sea, to claim a bloodship with their tribes of old: they—spell-bound, waited on his word....

Then as the years rolled on, and their head chief was dead, they shouted with one voice to make him Emperor....

O, Madog, from the land of Morning Star!

O, Quetzalcoatl, Bird serpent's[27] Conqueror!

Prince from Tlapallan!

Descendent of the gods!

Disseminator of knowledge!

Be our King!

---

27. Bird-serpent: griffin or dragon rouge, of Wales.

chapter XIII

"the god quetzalcoatl"

S O the annals go, and then are silent. The mists of time rise up, obscuring subsequent events, and tell not of the fate of those Welsh pioneers to Western seas.

To us, come but dim legends, gleaned by the the conquering Spaniards, when first they set their feet upon those self-same shores; tales which even then were fast crystallizing to mythology.

Thus runs the story which the Indians told.

Long years ago, in the time of our forebears, reigned over the country of Mexico, a God-King called Quetzalcoatl. The winds were his servants, the Singing Birds followed in his train!

Ah, it was good for the Aztec, when the Bird Serpent ruled o'er them!

For three score years he ruled o'er them!

Then came the Evil Spirit, Tezatlipoca. Tezatlipoca, his rival!

Spirit of Night, Spirit of Darkness!

Creeping down from the heavens, creeping, crawling along
on the web of a spider!

Coming in guise of a friend—to confer immortality upon
Quetzalcoatl!

Creeping, crawling, came Tezatlipoca!

And mixed him a magic potion, throwing in a few drops
of insidious poison!

Just a few drops, which created a thirsting—a great thirsting and longing for home!

Ah uncontrollable longing!

Alas! alas!

So potent the poison! So irresistible the longing … None
could withstand it!

Shaking as if with palsy—Quetzalcoatl—rose up; … the
Lord of Tlapallan arose! … at the call of his homeland!

Rose up, as it gripped at his vitals!

And in anguish he thundered,

"Make ready my vessels."

And his sign was the Star of the Morning!

Like the Star, he had come, rising up from the East.

In the dark he departed—some sixty—years after!

Two ships.. now ancient and sea-worn, set sail in the
gloaming … passed into the night … through the

darkness; and when day came ... behold they had vanished!

A cry went up from the sea-shore, where thousands of Aztecs were watching...

For—behold—Their god had passed from them!

But they said, "Some day he returns."

For centuries waited and watched and then came the Spaniards; and rushing joyful. to meet them, they cried, "Come ye from the land of Tlapallan?"

chapter xiv

"Chus madog slept"

I N the shade of a fisherman's hut, on the rocky Basque coast, an old man was lying, propped up with rude cushions.

So old and worn he was, that he appeared hardly still of this world.

His face, like dried parchment, seamed with wrinkles, which spread like a spiker-web, atwixt and athwart it. His grey beard flowed untrimmed across his breast; the white hair shagging down from forehead to eyebrows.

On the table near him, stood a writing horn, quill and parchment.

For a few minutes—with great effort—he would collect his thoughts … scrawl a short sentence … then lie back again, resting, with closed eyes.

Two months ago, Madog (for it was he) and his companions of the *Annesta*, had sighted land, after long weeks of buffeting at sea. Then a thick fog descending upon them, blotted out the world. Thus in their blindness, they were carried by strong tides upon the rocky shores of Cantabria.

The old ship soon went to pieces, and but three of her crew were saved. Madog, with both ankles broken, was washed ashore; and as a corpse he lay, amongst the sea-weed on the beach, till found by a woman seeking drift-wood, one Jeanne of Benzol, who summoning help, had him carried to her cot, where ever since he'd lain ... she tending him. His countrymen, his fellows in misfortune, soon found his whereabouts, and stayed to watch beside him for two dreary months.

Then coming to his ears, that from a neighbouring port, a ship was soon to sail for English shores, he begged so earnestly that they would go ... and take a message ... that if perchance his Gwenllian were yet alive, she might have news of him....

(How often had he watched their hungry eyes gaze northwards towards that land of which their fathers spoke ... the land for which they had embarked, and face such perils to arrive!)

For long they argued—they could not leave him in his weakness.

But ever answer came from Madog, "Few days, I shall be weak ... then casting off this feeble chrysalis, which here you see, soar gleaming through the clouds! But you, who if you should miss this barque, may waste a life of years upon this alien soil, when all your heart blood cries for Wales! Think not to be ungrateful, or unkind. I beg you, pray you, *order* you to go."

And so, with many turnings, and much glancing back, at last they left the fishing hut where Madog lay, questioning if they did right.

🎵 🎵 🎵

And so it fell one early autumn morn, the Lord Madog lay within the shadow, and he dozed and wrote, and wrote and dozed again, stringing together—bit by bit—the story of the finding that great land again.

"Which had so long been parted from the east ... lost ever since the time of Nöe's flood, but which the Druids never had forgot;—for had not Celtic forebears launched their dead, hoping to reach the old nest of their race! but he, he Madog, had made a track across the sea, planting the men of Gwallia ... *living* men, and left them as the ruling race ... and there his bones had lain (beneath some gilded pyramid perhaps), if this strange longing for his boyhood's home, had lured him not, in his decrepit age, to start a

journey, which cruel circumstance had ended here! ... but"
... and then, he wrote again ... how slowly moved the pen,
how danced the words before his filming eyes ... as halt-
ingly he ended thus his scrip—

"And here I lie," he scrawled, "a wreck which once was
a man, hopeless and helpless ... and the home ... to which
I speed is not amongst the mountains!" ... He closed his
eyes, to see again the hoary brow of Idris in his dreams, to
hear the rumble of the surf 'neath Aberffraw ... then—
came a rush of wings ... which opening, he perceived a
flock of pigeon flying north atwixt the mainland and the
sea ... he smiled ... and sighed.

Thus Jeanne de Benzol found him, his pen just falling
from his hand, his page still wet...

So she, and Renan, her 'bon homme' wrapped him
within his cloak ... and buried him ... midst many prayers
within the garden of St. José's church, and paid the priest
two white milch-goats to say a weekly mass for his departed
soul.

Beside him, in an old stone crock, sealed down, secure
from damp, they placed his precious manuscript; and up
above his head, planted a sapling yew ... had he not said,
"he loved the yews, for many grew in Wales!" For the Lord
Madog spoke a language like the old Cantabrian tongue, or
many words were like.

And thus, within the whisper of the surf, a Prince of Gwynedd lay; where the salt breeze came sobbing through the grass, where spray was thrown on stormy days … and where, in winter time, the sea mists rose and spread their coverlet of filmy whiteness over him. Thus, Madog slept, and dreamed!

END OF THE FIRST BOOK

book 11

chapter 1

"a cantabrian folk tale"

"AH bah! little baggage, so thou wouldst bribe thy old nurse for a tale; never hath she a moment's peace when thou art near, Holy Mary! 'A story Nanna, a story Nanna!' ever the same cry! … Well, eat thy supper, little one, … but open thy mouth as well as thine eyes … I vow, it would rather have dragons than honey for supper, this mannikin of mine!" babbled Giovanna, roguishly pinching the wistful little face turned up to hers "Well, the 'Dragon story' let it be … now eat … thou need'st not listen with thy mouth stupid!"

"Once, very long ago …" she began impressively, "in a savage country—far across the sea— lived a beautiful Prince, but he had a foot that was malformed, and they would not make him King … nevertheless he married a beautiful Princess, and was happy, till his brother (tempted by Satan) … slew her, then was his home hateful to him, and he despised his country of his birth. So entering his ship he sailed away across the ocean, far … far away, to the uttermost parts of the world, where storms for ever rage, and waves rise higher than Apennines. …" She paused for breath.

"Then, after many days, tossed by sea-tempests, and in much distress … when hope was lost, he reached a wondrous continent where birds were of the rainbow hue, where rivers ran with silver, where all the sand is gold! Where grow such fruits—as eat the saints in Paradise— where tree trunks ooze with honey, where shines the sun as it once shone in Eden … ere our first parents fell." … Giovanna sighed. "But eat thy bread, little one, *I* will cease," she continued menacingly, "if *thou* dost not continue!"

"Well, well … for many years the Prince ruled this blest land, the people of the place took him even for their God! But, ah … a-lack-and-a-well-a-day … when he was growing old, the Evil One appeared, and sighed into his ear the sigh of his own country, till he grew sick with longing … and then, he manned his ship, and sailed away … But ah! he never reached his home. For faith, the sea gods carried him upon the northern coasts of Spain, and sank his galleon not half a mile from my old home! … ah, dear Basque home," sighed Vanna, a mist of tears gathering in her dark eyes. "But!" brushing them away with work-soiled hand—"but, still at lowest tide, thou may'st behold the reef even to-day; they call it 'Dragon rocks,' because the crest he carried was a Dragon Rouge, a-carved and painted on his vessel's prow; and all were drowned," she continued, "but three. The Prince himself was washed ashore much hurt, but living still, a fisherwoman found and cared for him … until he died … not many Saints' days afterwards, but ere he died, he ciphered in a magic hand, the story of his voyage. …

"Drink they milk, little one!" bringing her fist down with a bang, till all the platters danced, "drink thy milk, never wilt thou grow big, or go to sea. I'll tell no more till all is done, my gutter snipe!"

"O Vanna, do not stop, I will drink all."

"That is the end, Babino; a great yew tree marks the place where they buried him, in God's garden at St. José … they say … that he wrote much before he died, and what he wrote is buried with him … they say the Dragon Rouge lies with it, 'twixt his paws! they say" … she whispered fearsomely, "that none dare steal it, whilst his master sleeps … *I* know the spot! … the wise ones say" … her voice dropped till it was almost inaudible, "that when a storm is brewing, he rises from his grave and walks all night, his Dragon following— like a hound … all night he walks … the wind's cries, like his dead companions' groans! … then ever follow wrecks … and corses buried in St. José's yard! They do say" … continued the woman, growing pale, "the Dragon digs them up and sucks their blood … Babino, go to bed!" shouted Giovanna shaking her charge, "and do not cry if thou awake, or I shall smack thee soundly!" then determinately snatching up the child, the old nurse hastily began to undress the four year old son of Domenico Columbus.

"But, Vanna," whispered he stroking the wrinkled cheek, "tell me, beautiful Vanna, that which thou saidst about the Dove!"

"Oh, bless the child! … thou wilt ever have thy stories the same … 'tis but an old crone's saw, 'That one day when the world should be grown old, a Dove should fly from Spain, and crossing many seas should reach the Dragon's lair, and pluck a palm wreath for the Spanish King' … Old woman's saws, old woman's saws … truth they have nothing else to do but talk! Now," putting the boy into his cot, "thou must *not* wake, or waking, must not scream, or Vanna's clout shall make thy young hide twinge!"

"Vanna," said the child, putting his arms round her neck, "shall I some day go and see the Dragon Rouge?"

"Yes simpleton, if thou eat every night thy supper well; only brave boys approach the yew!"

chapter 11

"The Treasure of the Crock"

TWENTY years later ... a man dismounted at the door of the only inn of San José. It was an autumn evening, the first bite of winter chilled the air.

From the little chapel on the hill, came the clang of the vesper bell, ringing rancourously ... insistently, the iron tongue seemed saying "Come to church, come to church, come to church ... or be damned, or be damned!" He appeared to be a sea-faring man ... evidently a stranger to the place—he stood a moment, looking around ... then hammered with his whip-handle on the Auberge door.

Mine host opened it, drying his hands on his apron.

The traveller explained to him, he wanted lodgings for himself and horse ... the landlord shook his head, muttered a few words in Basque, then turned and called to some one within—

"Ferdinand, Ferdinand!" Presently a man, a muleteer, emerged from the inside darkness. He was a Spaniard, and addressed the traveller in that language.

"Spanish is Dutch to him," he remarked politely, pointing his thumb over shoulder at his host.

Columbus—for it was he—threw him the reins and entered the rush-strewn kitchen. He signed for wine and food ... sat down upon the bench, stretching out his legs, which were still with riding.

Presently the muleteer returned from stabling his mount, and he invited him to come and drink and talk while he was eating, at which, the ever thirsty carrier seemed nothing loath.

And whilst he drank, Columbus questioned him, about himself ... his work ... and then about the neighbourhoud.

"How came you here? You are not of *these* parts, my good man; no dam or sire of the Basque country ever gave you birth."

"Oh no, Señor, I am of the Spanish blood ... good Spanish blood, from Andalusia, but I am wedded to a woman of this place, and here I live and work and partner with her father; for we have mules, and trade across the mountains, carrying produce to and fro ... but 'tis beggar's work." He lifted the flagon to his lips and drank a draught, wiped the back of his hand across his mouth, and sighed with pleasure.

"To your good health, Señor! all blessings of the Saints be yours. ... You come from far?"

"I? I have no home, the ocean my broad acres, my latest ship my house ... I am a mariner ... as hard a life as yours, good Ferdinand."

"What brought you here to these rude shores—if 'tis not boldness on my part to ask?"

"Not much ... I travel for amusement ... this time for folly ..." he paused and watched the muleteer's eye ever growing brighter under the influence of the unwonted flagon of Oporto.

"Once, when I was a little boy ... I heard a fairy-tale ... and it pleased me, in passing near San José to see if there were any truth in the old legend!" He shrugged his shoulders. "They said, that once a shipwrecked prince was buried here, and near him in a crock, a parchment, that he penned, about some distant countries ere he died!"

"Oh, Dragon Rouge?" said Ferdinand with a broad smile, "that old gammer's tale! which goodwives frighten fractious babies with! ha! ha! ... ha! ha!" he laughed till the rafter echoed back his merriment.

"Then you have heard it too?"

"Heard it? O blest St. Catherine, have I heard my father sneeze? 'tis common talk! told to the infants yet unswathed—when first they trot, their mothers walk them round the yew, and when they cry at nights, 'The Prince with his red Dragon waits for thee!' and quickly hush their mewing."

"Then all men know ..." He paused ... then ventured ... "Has any ever attempted digging on the spot, to test the truth?"

"O Holy Mary ... 'twere basest sacrilege; only with bared heads we venture near!" said the man crossing himself.

"Do you care for money, my good Ferdinand?" said the stranger tentatively, leaning across the table, and speaking in a lower voice.

"Little enough I ever had to try!" answered the muleteer, scratching his head, "yet, sir, what hungry peasant ever turned away, at ring of blest piaster 'neath his hand!"

"Well, Ferdinand, if you will help me in my venture, I'll give you five doubloons, five gold doubloons ... and ever and a day you shall drink best of wine ... your wife wear ribbons and your children shoes! not much I ask, but—I have a fancy to discover for myself, if this dead prince lies really there, and if beneath his head is placed the crock, and in the crock, the manuscript he wrote! Now will you be my man?"

"Ah, Sire!" Ferdinand sprang up, his face radiant, knocking over in his excitement his now empty flagon. "Ah, Sire!" then the pleasure slowly faded, "but," he paused, "they say, *he* laid a curse on whomsoever should disturb his rest ...

and then … the Dragon, Sire!" In the glow of the rushlight Columbus saw a sickly whiteness creep across his face!

"Tut .. tut … you are a craven fool!"

"Ah, Señor—let me ask my wife?"

"All right, poor man, be off and ask your master. And I will go and wanter round the church, ere it grows quite dark, and see the spot. But stay," he laid a detaining hand on his shoulder, "should you fail to receive dispensation, lay me a pick and spade and lanthorn, near the yew … and I will give you *one* doubloon; but, if you dare be brave, then meet me when the moon is risen full a quarter after two."

Amidst the scurrying clouds the great pale lunar orb was sailing pompously. A man wrapped in a riding cloak, stepped quietly out of the side door of the San José Inn, and started walking towards the little chapel on the hill, which lay between the village and the sea.

Rapidly he climbed the path leading to the consecrated ground … and passing through the wicket, went in the direction of the yew which stood out darkly in the moonlight.

There was no one there … no sound save the swish of the sea below, as it ground the pebbles in its intermittent rushes.

When he reached the yew, he commenced groping around in the shadow; presently he found a spade, a pick and lanthorn, which latter he lit.

Without further waiting, he began to dig.

How many roots this cursed yew-tree had.

Cutting first one and then another with his dagger, he continued digging ever down and down ... now, he was quite four feet from the surface ... surely he must be getting near.

How hot it was! he took off his doublet; he drank a long draught from his water gourd ... then recommenced with renewed vigour.

Shovel after shovel full of earth he threw up ... then handled his pick again ... at last! After some two hours' work, it hit a resisting surface ... he put his hands down, and groping in the soft mould brought up, an earth-stained skull ... he held it to the light, how like to blood the stain ... for a minute the desecration of his act gripped him with fear ... but ... after all this disturbing of the dead was but for the benefit of the living!

He placed it carelessly on the grass above ... to recommence his digging. And now, after a few minutes his spade touched something hard ... only a stone perchance ... but the tap-roots seemed to have grown round it, and like the tentacles of an octopus were jealous of their prey ... he cut each root in turn ... then put his pick beneath ... and straining every muscle prised it up.

It was an earthen crock … he split it with his spade … then on his hands and knees, by the flickering lanthorn light, he tore out the contents.

Tightly sewn, within a goat-skin, he found a parchment, and a quaint rough map. … Climbing out of his pit … with trembling fingers he spread out the scroll upon a neighbouring mound … but the moon was dimmed by passing clouds, and he could not see the words … but he had all he sought. Giovanna's fairytale was true, and he had found the key that proved his theory that the earth was round, the key that unlocked the long-guessed route to the rich lands of Marco Polo's days! for if land lay to west it *must* be India.

As quickly as he could, he re-shovelled in the earth again and stamped it down. Then feeling in his girdle, he drew out his purse, taking therefrom a doubloon, placed it inside the lanthorn frame: and hid the precious scrip within his breast, put on his jerkin and his cloak.

Descending the hill, he hurried back towards the inn.

There he left money for "mine host," and saddling his horse rode through the silent moonlit land, towards the Cantalabrian hills again … and as day dawned, blessed all the saints that he had safely reached their fastness.

During the day he rested in a cave, for fear of pursuit, feeding himself on berries and black bread, whilst his stallion browsed the herbage of the banks. Tired as he was, worn out for want of sleep … he took the precious packet from his coat, and laid it on the sun-baked rock … scanning it, first from one side, then another … but not one single word could he decipher.

"The magic writing!" he sighed, his face drawn with the disappointment.

Next day he reached a convent of Franciscan Friars … and bode that night.

And after supper—whilst in converse with the Brothers—made mention of a document that he had brought, and bet ten pistolés to one, no Friar there could read the writ!

Some of the more learned tried … but each man failed … Columbus won his bet … and lay down in the guest chamber most disconsolate, to sleep … holding the key to all his hopes … but unable to decipher any word of it!

So months went on … he made a tour of learned schools, but none could help him read.

At last, he put away his parchment baffled, returning to Madrid—his hopes which once ran high, now trailed along the ground.

Then, when expecting least a strange thing happened. … It was a tavern brawl at "Inn Toledo"; a stranger was being roughly handled, and Columbus took his part, and hitting right and left, saved him from killing; and binding up his cuts carried him home … poor boy … his head was badly broke … he bore him up the stairs to his small room (which lay beneath the tiles) in one of the back streets of Madrid City.

Laying him on his bed, he bathed his wounds, and watched him through the night, tending him—lavishing what salves a poor man's purse could furnish.

A week went by, the invalid grew better ... and Columbus, ever working at his charts (his only means of livelihood) began to question him; and ask him of his business in the Capital.

"My name," answered the man in broken Spanish, "is Maurice Lloyd, a student of Oxford town, who would study the operations of the laws of different countries ... and the histories thereof; and when I study not ... which happens oft ..." he said with a smile, "I amuse myself collecting songs, and turning them to Welsh. I have a pretty ear for verse, and make new songs to sing." Then after a pause ... "I come from Wales," proudly, "the King of England now, is of our stock, a son of Owen Tudor ... you've heard of him no doubt?"

"Oh, yes, a noted monarch your Welsh Henry, some day I may go suppliant to his Court, for he can help me much, I have no doubt. ... Say ... being such a traveller do you speak many tongues?"

"No, mighty few ... only mine own, and English ... and Latin ... precious small .. but tell me why you ask?"

Columbus hesitated, ... then tentatively—

"Because I have a manuscript, which none may read … one I found months ago. … Many wise men have tried, but failed, 'tis writ in some strange jargon, but look! perchance, it *may* be Welsh, although I have small faith … but if you will but cast your eye across the page …"

From under his bed Columbus dragged a brass-bound box, unlocking which, he took with care—wrapped in its hide covering—his precious document; and unrolling it, he laid it before the student.

Maurice scanned it attentively for a few minutes … then looking up at the waiting man, in surprise!

"Holy Mary! in the name of Heaven, where did you get this from? Indeed, indeed," as he traced his finger along the closely written lines, "Lord love us, for 'tis all in Welsh … old Welsh … old Welsh … but quite decipherable … I will try and read it, and doubt me not I may succeed."

Then with wrinkled brow and halting speech, he began … translating each sentence as he went …

"I, Madog, true son of Owain, King of Gwynedd, before I go to meet my Judge, sit down—(ere death shall clinch my fingers in his own)—to write the story of my life beyond the seas.

"Whereas in the year of our Lord 1170, the King my father passed away, I, Madog disinherited through an infirmity of the foot, set aside (except for a small him patrimony), was cruelly wronged in the person of my

wife Annesta, by my most unnatural brother Davydd.
Tired of a life of bloodshed and rapine in Wales, I sailed,
with ten ships and three hundred men, towards a country
much recited in the annals of our Druids, a distant world,
which legend pointed, lay towards the west; which, after
thirteen weeks, battered, famished and disheartened, at last
we chanced upon. There for twice thirty years I and my
people dwelt, in happiness and peace, possessing wealth
and kind, not dreamt upon in hungry Gwallia! A land it
was of gold and silver, and plenteous fruitfulness, of balmy
air,—where grows, sans labour, corn and wheat and rye, yet
where the hunter finds much game, and fishers need but
cast their nets to catch a shoal. A land of milk and honey,
a very paradise. And yet … with all prosperity … as life
began to near its end for me, a cloud of wildest longing
darkened my horizon, and my heart thirsted once again to
see the barren mountains of my youth—and hold within
my arms the form of one I loved, more than aught else
… if still she lived, my daughter Gwenllian. Discoursing
thus, I so inflamed some of my compatriots with wish for
home, that sixty of my comrades—some, alas, as ancient
as myself! made sail, and ventured eastwards in our ship
again. But after many weeks of goodly weather, even as
we draw near the goal of our anticipation, a thick fog fell
upon the sea, and we lost reckoning, and on the third day
drifted on to rocks, and our good ship was ripped from

"and died in Spain. I've heard the tale before, 'tis written … or somewhat of the same, within the chronicles of Strata Florida."

That night, well-mended, the feckless student left his host, with many grateful thanks.

The evening air blew upwards from the street, Columbus sitting at his window gazing down upon the passing crowds below, sank on his knees,

"Santa Maria," he murmured, crossing himself fervently, "to-night I hold, in this my human hand, the key I've sought so long—now of a certainty I know, there lies a country to the west and I feel sure that 'tis the land of the Great Khan—and not by perilous adventure and years of travel slow, in future shall be brought the riches of the East to Spain, but by a few weeks sailing fair, at sea! Mother of Stars, the finding of this manuscript thou hast thyself directed, and thou thyself wilt guide me in the quest, unto these realms, and then, dear Mother mine—yes, there I'll spread thy name and that of thy great Son, (which to the heathen hordes shall be as dew on parching land). Christ and His Church shall reach triumphant round the world, where'er the sun shall rise, shall rise His followers to praise His name!"

And thus it came to pass … The Dragon Rouge of Wales, bequeathed unto the Spanish Dove (though all unwittingly) the knowledge treasured long, by a great Celtic race.

FINIS

Note.—Columbus was of opinion that nought but the Atlantic Ocean lay between Spain, and the East Indies, Carthay, and the land travelled by Marco Polo! He did not search for a new Continent, only a shorter route to one already known.

EDITOR'S NOTE

In the present iteration, our endeavour has been directed towards
maintaining utmost fidelity to the original text.

about the author

Joan Dane is a clever anagram of the widely used place-holder name, Jane Doe.

It is believed that Joan Dane is the pen name of Edwardian writer Mary Stuart Boyd (née Kirkwood).

Born in 1860 in Glasgow, Mary Stuart Boyd had a long career as a journalist and author. In 1880, she married Alexander Stuart Boyd, a famous painter whose illustrations are found in many of her works: *Our Stolen Summer* (1900), *Versailles Christmastide* (1901), *Prince Madog* (1909), and *The Forgotten Isles* (1911).

They had one son, Stuart Boyd, who later died of his wounds in World War I.

Mary and Alexander emigrated to Auckland, New Zealand, where they spent the rest of their lives.